BEAUTIFUL BEASTS

A COLLECTION OF VISCERAL HORROR

JAE MAZER

FEATHERED
TENTACLE PRESS

For Dad. I love you.

Whoever fights monsters should see to it that in the process he does not become a monster. And if you gaze long enough into an abyss, the abyss will gaze back into you.

— FRIEDRICH NIETZSCHE

CONTENTS

GOODBYE, BETHANY CHAMBERS

I love you.

Bethany thought it, but didn't say it. She didn't need to. She looked into her lover's eyes—glacier-blue, brimming with tears and tainted red with the memory of tears already shed. Their love could go unspoken. Regardless of words passing lips, it was there. After a decade of marriage, the strength of their affection and adoration had not waned. They knew. Bethany didn't need to say it aloud.

"I love you," Alice said, stroking Bethany's cheek.

Bethany melted into Alice's touch, the smoothness of her skin, the warmth of her longing. Gooseflesh fluttered over her body, and her heart swelled. But her stomach. Deep in the pit of her gut she felt not infatuation or desire, but dread. Doom. The understanding that Alice didn't need to say she loved her, and that was in fact not what she said. She had said goodbye.

Bethany didn't speak. She nodded and broke Alice's gaze, training her eyes on the building ahead instead. Brick and glass, cold and menacing. It waited for her, that reaper's abode, the patiently waiting turnstile to hell. It housed hundreds in limbo, those steeped in fear and supposition of how they would eventually leave its habitation.

Bethany knew how she would be leaving.

She took Alice's hand and squeezed, staring down their fate like prey at a predator.

"Sign here," the nurse said as walked around Alice to hand the clipboard to Bethany. Alice's swallow was audible — a heart wrenching gulp that punctuated the consent to kill on the paper in Bethany's hand.

"Ladies."

Bethany and Alice turned to the newcomer.

"Doctor Biron," Bethany said, dipping her head in a slight nod. Alice did not look at him, instead studying the pink laces on her Chuck Taylors.

Dr. Biron sat next to Bethany's bed and weaved his arm around the IV tubing and oxygen sensor. "How are you feeling, Mrs. Chambers?"

Like I'm courting death, and she's right wet and ready for me, Bethany thought, a smile teasing her lips.

"Surprisingly calm," Bethany admitted, looking sheepishly at the emotional rollercoaster that was her loving wife.

"That's perfectly normal," Dr. Biron said, resting his hand atop Bethany's.

"Acceptance." The words were hidden in Bethany's heavy breath, but were not missed by anyone in the eerie quiet of the pre-op room.

"No," Alice said, the word sharp and direct. "We accept nothing yet, my love."

"I'm just being realistic," Bethany said.

Cancer. Throat, lungs, God knows what else. The plan was to remove the big tumor that wrangled her breath and ability to swallow, then let the chemical cocktail of chemo wage war with the rest, see who rises victorious: Bethany or the Black Beast. Bethany's throat tightened as she thought about the months of agonizing recovery, of tracheotomy breathing, feeding tubes, pain, nausea... strangely enough, she longed for the adversity of those nuisances. In all likelihood, she wouldn't make it long enough to experience them.

"Bethany, let's focus on the positives," Dr. Biron said, false reassurance sweetening his words. "I wouldn't perform this surgery if I didn't have some hope of success."

You have to say that, Bethany thought, giving the young surgeon the once over. *If you didn't operate on someone my age, you'd be a monster amongst your peers, my friends, my family; thirty-two is too young to be left to crumble to dust.*

"How long will she be... out?" Alice asked, her eyes finally shifting to meet Biron's.

"The surgery itself will be lengthy— twenty hours or more. Then a few hours in recovery, and she'll be transferred to the ICU. You can wait for her there."

Dr. Biron's words dissolved into the air as he droned on, talking about outcomes and procedures. Alice nodded while her eyes glazed over. Bethany stilled her mind, thinking of nothing but her lover's touch, the feeling of her hand, the way her tousled hair was resting on her collarbone. Bethany was resigned to her fate, and would leave the world with nothing but love in her thoughts.

"I love you."

Bethany said it. Alice said it too.

Goodbye.

That's what it was, after all.

"I'll join you later," Alice said, her eyes fixed on Bethany's.

Sure.

A portly nurse shuffled into the room, pushing a stainless steel tray peppered with needles, packages, vials.

The anesthesiologist swooped in, describing sensations, procedures, timelines.

Bethany heard none of it.

She looked at Alice, right into her, and the love was enough to splinter her into a million pieces. Alice leaned forward, tear-drenched lashes dripping droplets on Bethany's pallid cheek. Bethany's mood lightened and heart fluttered as the delicate skin of Alice's peach lips pressed against hers, the wet pressure of her kiss sealing her fate.

Then Alice was gone.

Replaced by the clinking and clanking of medical tools, supplies of pain and repair.

"It's all right, dear," the nurse said, her voice fat and friendly. "Shall all be over soon. Waiting is the worst part."

Bethany nodded, attempting to conjure a smile for the kindly woman, a nurse wrapped in a mother's tenderness.

The anesthesiologist walked over to the bed, lifted Bethany's chart to his rounded faced, and shifted his Harry Potter specs to the end of his crooked nose to study the information within. After mumbling incoherent algorithms to himself, he gathered and loaded a syringe, injecting the beginning of Bethany's end into her IV line.

Bethany sighed, soft sobs shuddering from strained lungs, and resigned herself to her fate.

Lights.

Muted and yellow.

Flickering fast, faster, clipping through Bethany's eyelids at a manic pace.

The squeak-screech-squeaking of wheels beckoned to Bethany like an ailing ghoul.

"Where... what..."

The anesthetic was a dense cloud resting on Bethany's mind, seeping into the folds of her brain. She tried to reverse her blink, to open her eyes, but her lids were half-tonne cotton sealed against Gobi-dry eyes. She reached out, searching for something, for anything, trying to get a grip on her surroundings. Her fingers wrapped around the steel bedrail, cold and sterile, vibrating under the movement of the gurney. She slid her fingers along the metal until they brought up solid on something warm. Something hard and leathery. It recoiled from her touch, and the gurney clanked to a stop.

"Not yet." Bethany heard the nurse's voice, but it was not motherly or warm as it had been before. It was...

The jiggling of Bethany's IV line signaled her next descent into darkness.

BETHANY DRIFTED INTO CONSCIOUSNESS, her head muddy and mouth coated in the paste of sleep. She drew a deep breath through her nose, bracing herself for the post-op ache, but the air passed freely; her breath came smooth, without throbbing, stabbing, or any discomfort whatsoever. She opened her eyes, but her vision was milky. *Gorked out on pain meds, I suppose.* She lifted a hand to rub away the film so she could have a look at herself.

Her hand jarred mere centimeters from its resting place on the bed.

Restraints.

She struggled against the leather straps.

Her ankles were restrained, too.

What?

"Awake are we, dear?"

The portly nurse.

"What happened?" Beth asked. "Why am I restrained? Where's Alice?"

"Now, now dear," the nurse cooed. "Don't work yourself into a tizzy. It will be all right soon. All over soon."

Bethany blinked hard, trying to clear the veil of film from her sight. The room was dim, dimmer than a recovery room should have been. And yellow. The lights glowed a spooky amber, and the walls were dark. Ceiling too. And the smell. Musty, damp...

"Where am I?"

Bethany was startled by a touch on her foot. She craned her neck, and saw a figure looming between her legs, hands on her ankles. The hands moved up and down her calves, warm and slick, as if covered in oil.

"Who…"

Bethany became acutely aware of her nudity. The fine hairs on her body stood at attention, grasping at every breath and breeze that passed around the room. Her nipples were erect, her flesh cold. The warm liquid felt nice, save its mystery.

"Stop," she said, voice weak and pleading.

The hands didn't stop. They worked their way up one thigh then the other, massaging, sliding, kneading. They moved onto her arms, working her from shoulder to fingertip. Then her torso, her neck, her face, her scalp. The hands kept grinding, pushing, squeezing until Bethany's entire body was sore and thick with whatever manner of slime the stranger had applied.

"What…"

Another jiggle of the IV tube.

Another plunge into darkness.

Four more times.

Four more times Bethany woke, her body worked over with the mystery oil before she was sent back to the darkness.

Another pair of hands helped, two sets in total, massaging and kneading her raw. She couldn't focus, couldn't steady her mind from the pharmaceutical cocktail pumping through her veins, but she heard them. Their voices, menacing and deceitful. Dr. Biron and the nurse, laughing, chit-chatting as if they were milling about the water cooler rather than repeatedly assaulting her. *Dodgy wankers.*

Her mind drifted to Alice. Her laugh, her smell, the soft squish of her body when they were pressed together under their cave of a duvet. The way her hair reached out like a birch broom in the fits as she poured their morning coffees. The way she made her completely, intoxicatingly at peace.

BETHANY LOST count of how many times Biron and the nurse had come. She was present and aware for only brief glimpses of time in that windowless chamber, unable to catch the rise and fall of moon or sun, not knowing whether minutes, weeks, or months had passed. Occasionally they would leave her awake for a spell, giving her the opportunity to examine herself and her surroundings. A room with cinderblock walls and a floor of dirt, table and chairs in the corner, medical tools on rotting wooden counters lining the walls. Yellowed bulbs sputtered in crusted sconces hanging off the walls. The smell of dirt and must coated the insides of her nostrils, summoning a gag.

A basement. A cellar.

They would dine at the table, Doctor Biron and the nurse, cutlery clanking, the sound less than half as sharp as their voices; voices that seared in Bethany's brain, boiling a rage only yet teasing to erupt.

Does Alice know I'm gone? Is she searching for me? Does she have any idea?

Hot tears streamed down Bethany's cheeks, seeping into the pillow below her soaked and oily head. Panic sank its claws into her heart as she imagined herself and Alice at that table, dining on their favourite fare of tapas and merlot, Bette Davis Eyes playing on a crackling turntable in the background. Her mouth watered.

Will I taste my life again?

Garbled snarling.

Suction.

The sound of wet, heavy... chewing?

Bethany turned her head to the side, squinting through the drug fog, and spotted the duo sitting at the table in the corner, hunched over, furiously working away at their meal. Bethany squinted her eyes, straining to see her captors. Bethany's restraints rattled as she shifted on the bed, and the nurse turned her head.

"Mornin' dear."

Meat, sinewy and shredded, hung from the nurse's lower lip, swaying to and fro, glistening in sauce and saliva. The doctor raised his head too, and even though the room was two shades from the hue of midnight, Bethany could see crimson smeared and gleaming across his face. He sucked his fingers one by one, greedily consuming the meal's leavings coating each digit.

"Oh God," Bethany gasped.

She knew.

"You... mean to... you can't eat me."

The nurse and Doctor Biron cocked their heads like perplexed canines.

'What's that now, Bethany?" Doctor Biron said, his tone professional and placating.

Fucking cannibals, Bethany screamed, words silent on the wings of stolen breath.

The nurse stood and walked over to Bethany, her great body heaving with every step. Doctor Biron joined her, standing on the opposite side of the bed. Bethany started when the nurse loosened the restraint on her left arm.

"No funny business, sweetheart," the nurse said. "Jus' a quick exam."

The nurse lifted Bethany's arm, limp from chemical restraint, and pinched the soft flab of flesh between her elbow and armpit. Bethany winced, anticipating pain, but felt very little.

"I need you to believe, Bethany," Doctor Biron said, "that we are here to help you. We mean you no harm."

The nurse clasped the restraints back on Bethany's wrist. She slid her hands down Bethany's ribcage and squeezed the meager flesh on her abdomen, pulling it away from her body. Bethany howled in pain as flesh and tendon and muscles separated from her ribcage as the nurse hauled her skin into the air. After an excruciating moment, the nurse released her grasp, and pressed Bethany's flesh back against her bones.

"Hmmm," the nurse hummed through pursed lips. "Woulda thought you bush-munchers would be easier."

"Excuse me?" Bethany said.

The nurse leaned in, her chapped, cracked lips millimeters from Bethany's ear. "Moist," the nurse cooed, her thick, meaty tongue teasing the fronts of her brown teeth. "I expected you to be more moist."

Bethany thrashed against her restraints, screaming and hollering, spittle and oil splattering over the pale scrubs worn by Dr. Biron and the nurse.

SHE'S NOT READY.

She's close enough.

Should we wait?

We could, but she's resisting more and more.

The voices swelled into focus, rattling in Bethany's head, a taunting chorus of doom. As she floated out of unconsciousness, movement blurred around the sides of her hospital bed. More people now, moving rapidly, focused on tasks and duties Bethany could only imagine. Her skin itched and ached, the pervasive moisture causing her flesh to sag and wrinkle.

They're fucking basting me.

"You goddamn monsters," Bethany hissed through slippery lips.

The movement ceased for only half a breath, then continued its purposeful scurrying.

Bethany blinked and blinked, her hand instinctually rising to wipe the sludge from her eyes.

This time, her hand reached the target.

The restraints were gone.

Bethany didn't think. She leapt to her feet, but her legs gave way, muscles flubbery from lack of use. She hit the dirt, her face and hands sinking into the moist soil, and she flailed around, grasping for something to pull herself upright. Her fingers found purchase on cold metal. She gave a firm yank, toppling over the steel cart beside the hospital bed. She groped around the cart and let out a squeal of elation when her fingers found what they sought.

A scalpel, long and large and sharp.

She took a swipe, the blade slicing a wide swath through the air. "Stay back. Get away from me!"

The room was silent. All breath was held and movement ceased. Bethany rubbed at her eyes with the back of her hand, taking care not to cake herself with the soil on her palms.

"Bethany."

"No! Stay away!"

Bethany floundered like a fish until her back was against a wall, her predators placed in front of her, safely in her line of returning sight.

"I know you're scared, Bethany."

"I'm fucking pissed!" Bethany howled.

Bethany could finally see. She looked down at her body, and had to stifle the gorge in her throat. Her skin had become a glossy mush, moist and translucent. She poked at her stomach with a mud-coated finger and depressed the gooey flesh as if it were Jello.

Bethany finally looked. She looked up to her captors. Doctor Biron. The nurse. The others. It was them, but it wasn't. Creatures, dark green, iridescent scales glistening like oil in the faint light. Talons on rigid, skeletal fingers, elongated limbs that dragged on the floor as they swayed and loped their way around the room.

"Dear?"

A hefty creature with blood-brown eyes and a bloated chest gyrated towards her, kneeling down to her level on reverse articulated limbs.

"Dear, let me give you something."

Bethany swatted the needle out of the thing's grasp and swiped at its throat with the scalpel. The blade hit the creature's hide with a clank, failing to make even the tiniest nick.

"Bethany."

No...

"Bethany listen..."

A new voice from the far reaches of the room.

Fuck no, please no...

"There was no other way. You know that. There was no way out but death."

How... you...

"It was death... or change."

What?

"It was terminal, Bethany. A five percent chance. *Five percent*. Then the quality of life afterwards. The pain, the chemo, never tasting steak and wine again..."

As the creature spoke, approaching Bethany as if she were a frightened, abused puppy, a home movie played in Bethany's brain. Meeting Alice, their hands brushing together as they reached for the same novel at the library. That first date at the cheap Italian restaurant with the shitty wine and monster-sized portions. The first time they made love, clumsy and sensual. And every subsequent time, powerful and passionate; warm, tender, excruciatingly splendid. The ivory of their wedding, turning a house into a home. Life. Life assigned an imminent expiration date by a venomous, vile disease.

The creature was on its knees next to Bethany, its exposed, crimson bones pierced deep into the soil. It reached a taloned hand out and took the scalpel from Bethany's trembling grasp. Bethany watched her reflection in the blade as the creature pressed the steel to Bethany's forearm, piercing it deep into the moist flesh.

She felt nothing.

She didn't bleed.

Bethany watched as the creature plunged its talons into her translucent, jellied flesh, peeling away effortlessly, soaked and separated by the oil. And underneath that moistened skin wasn't bone and muscle and tendon, but scales, black and rippling and iridescent like oily rainbows.

Bethany looked up at the creature, into those icy blue eyes, and the warm panic of love filled her lungs.

"I love you," the creature said.

I love you.

THE WAIF AND THE WITCH

My cornflakes were soggy.

Ugly, I thought. *Artificial. Unnatural.*

I stared at the bowl, giving it a swirl with my rusted spoon, sending bits of flakes sloughing off into the ever-thickening sludge of breakfast soup.

"What's your problem, Taissa?" Saggy Jean asked, flicking milk on my dirt encrusted face. The thick, pert-near curdled droplets sludged down my cheek like infected tears.

"Oh, I dunno, Sags," Wilber said, rapping his battered knuckle on her shoulder. "What's there to be sour about, eh?"

I looked around. Fire from the pits cast dancing ghosts across the faces of the impending dead. Accents of garbage and graffiti decorated the concrete of the underpass. The wretched were perched upon blankets and ratty furniture stained with all manner of what had one time been inside one orifice or another. The humidity acted as a delivery agent for the smell of rancid crotch permeating the air that hung heavy over the shanty town.

Disgusting, what this place has become.

I stifled a gag and set my bowl of cornflakes on the ground by the fire.

"Wha's that?" Saggy Jean said, shifting her mono-boob over to the left side of her stomach.

"'Tis jus' a girl, that one," Wilber said, tilting his head towards my slouched-over, living carcass. "Leave 'er alone, wills ya?"

"Mhmm," Saggy Jean said, cocking a brow at me.

That's right, sow. Judge me. But I am here to help you. And help you I shall. All of you. Soon.

I smiled through matted webs of greasy hair, baring my teeth like dull fangs.

"Jus' a girl," Saggy Jean parroted, her voice communicating the disbelief in her own words. "Not that one, nah. Right bitch, she is."

Eye rolls flashed and snorts echoed around the underpass. The residents of the Shitty Shanty Walk were used to Saggy Jean's gripes and moans and accusations.

"They're all evil, Sags," Wilber said, clucking his tongue. "Those with breasts separate and skin not yet weathered like an ol' leather recliner. Leave the orphan be."

"I don't likes the look of 'er," Saggy Jean said, giving me the once over with an eye reeking of stench. "Ne'er did."

The smell of the dozen vagabonds and their belongings flooded my nose and throat, overpowering the odour of sour milk that had, until that point, been the dominating scent. Saliva pooled beneath my tongue, and I stifled the urge to gag as I rose from my seat on the upturned milk crate. I started to walk away, but Saggy Jean reached out and grabbed my forearm, digging her yellow nails into my pallid flesh.

"What's the matter, darlin'?" Saggy Jean asked. But there was no worry in those eyes.

"Leave her be," Wilbur scolded, swatting Saggy's hand and loosing my arm in the process.

Saggy opened her mouth to argue, but was cut off by the bemoaning of static and despair from an archaic radio perched upon a nearby brick.

... WITH LITTLE MORE TO GO ON than distraught family members waving missing persons reports, police are asking for assistance from anyone and everyone who may have seen anything suspicious in the past few weeks. With the disappearance of Leslie French, the count is up to eight in a few short months...

"PEDOPHILE," Wilber said, cracking his knuckles.

"'Taint that," a voice mumbled from under a mountain of swollen blankets. "Ain't no pedo killin' a thirty-year-old woman."

"We're not sure that anyone's dead," Wilbur said. "Jus' taken. Meddled with, I'm sure."

"Meddled, gutted, whatever," Rita said, emerging from her woolen cocoon.

"Funny, though, no trace," Wilber muttered to himself. "Something unnatural about that."

I stepped away from the group and headed towards the stairs at the side of the overpass.

"Not a smart thing, girl," Rita called after me, "goin your own way with the likes of that savage out there."

I turned, slitting my eyes and contorting my mouth into a humourless grin.

"Death is welcome here, I'm certain," I growled, and caressed my prepubescent body.

I faced my destination once more, clopping my logans up the filth covered steps. As I walked away, I could hear their whispers. Gossiping, judging.

"Well then," Rita said, turning to Wilber. "A right pleasant one she be."

"She be jus' a pup," Wilber said, a sigh coating his words. "Mudder fadder tossed me to the wind, I'd be sour too."

Saggy Jean said nothing, just watched me go as I left shadows of hate in my wake.

I raised my nose to the sky as soon as my feet hit the dirt, a scrap of land protected by imposing poplars that hovered above the garden like stoic sentries. I rounded the trees, dropped to my knees, and drove my fingers deep into the dirt. I balled my fists and squeezed the forgiving loam through my fingers.

Earth is beauty, beauty is earth.

I inhaled, drawing deep the scent of magnolia and hibiscus lingering in the breeze. I opened my eyes, drawing the curtain on a starlit production of petals, reds and whites and pinks, lavender vines reaching for me with emerald fingers.

"Beauty," I said, my breath escaping in tendrils of condensation in the cool night air.

A small huff of air crossed the backs of my ankles, grazing the flesh where the hole in my boot left me exposed. My head snapped towards the movement, and I came face to face with a puppy. A beagle, eyes saucers of warm chocolate and fur new and soft like velvet, whimpered for my touch, finding my hand and nuzzling it with its cold, wet nose.

Its long snout.

Altered and tainted by decades of breeding.

Ruined by human interference.

Terrible creatures.

"Hello, mutt," I cooed, stroking the pup's head. The pup

wagged its tail and snuggled into my stone embrace. I faked consolation for a moment before turning its face to mine. "You are filthy. Unnatural. And you smell."

The pup didn't yelp. It didn't cry out or so much as whimper when I held its skull in my dirt-coated fist and twisted its neck like a bottle cap. I lingered over my actions for a moment before fetching a box cutter from my pocket and flaying the pup on the ground before me. Once the beast's insides were on the outside, I plunged my hands back into the ground, squelching my fingers through layers of organs, tissues, blood, driving them deep into the earth and kneading together both dirt and death.

"Quite the green thumb."

The voice from behind me did not deserve my attention. I continued tilling soil with pup, turning and churning, kneading and pressing.

"I know you, bitch," Saggy Jean said, standing a safe distance away, watching from the blind of a senseless poplar. "I don't know what you are, but I'm onto you. You's got eve'yone fooled, but not me."

I stopped moving. I turned my head towards my portly neighbor and licked the air. *She tastes like fear and croissants,* I thought, stifling a giggle in my gut.

"You French?" I stuttered through a snicker.

"Pardon?" Saggy Jean said, tilting her head like a dog at a piccolo recital.

I laughed. I opened my mouth wide and let brays of

manic whooping drive Saggy Jean back from where she came. Once Saggy was over the bank and out of sight, my smile dissolved into a scowl, drooping my face and sinking my spirits.

So ugly.

That rancid cunt. Her smells, her sounds, the tacky damp-ness of her skin.

An example of the ruination of humankind.

It must be horrible being so vile.

A tear formed at the corner of my eye. I quickly swiped it away with a muddy bloody finger, damming the flow before it released.

"I'M SO HUNGRY, MA'AM."

I widened my eyes and heavied my pout, gently stroking the woman's hand with the tips of my fingers.

I coached myself. *Shy, demure, broken,* I thought, willing my face to convey the illusion.

"Oh, you poor thing," the woman said, scrounging in her purse for dredges of change. "How old are you, sweetheart? Where are your parents?"

"Gone, ma'am."

Silenced. By my hand after I took her. And now they are cleansed.

"Bloody sin," the woman said, shaking her head.

The real sin is your despair, I thought as I scanned the woman, her manicured nails, her perfectly preened hair, the exhaustion hidden beneath layers of makeup.

"Where do you live?" the woman asked, extending a five-dollar bill.

I did not take the money.

I did not want the money.

Money is not what I needed.

What I needed was for the world to be cleansed of filth and reborn to beauty, to its natural, intended state.

I turned and walked away, forcing dry, audible sobs from my throat.

The woman followed.

Like a lemming. I bet she lives her life that way, following orders, following the crowd and the rules and the madness, maintaining the status quo that shames and degrades others of our very own species.

Fucking disgraceful.

"Little girl?" the woman said as she trotted after me, her high heels clipping and clopping down the pavement until she crossed the street into the field where the dirt muted her footfalls. "Where are you going? Let me help you!"

No. Let me help you.

Soon, we were in my garden.

My pale skin was stained with streaks of crimson that shone black in the moonlight, coating my cheeks and arms and budding breasts. I stood naked, feet pressed into the damp soil, swaying with the wind. The trees blocked out the filth of the world, leaving me ignorant in my garden of solace, listening to the dirt suckle its new, wet meat.

"You are so much more beautiful this way," I told the woman under my feet.

... ANOTHER FOUR GONE MISSING in the past few months, brings the total to a staggering twelve. Police are canvasing the area for witnesses and evidence...

Slow. So slow, this cleanse. So many people, so much ugliness.

The radio mocked me, reminding me of the snail's pace of my task; hinting at the futility of the goal I had set for myself. I remembered my vow, a vow I made to myself years ago when I took her. A child, I thought, would be a better predator. No one would suspect a child. But children are slow and weak. They cannot lift and heave, they haven't the strength to fight, and the muscle it takes to flay, carve, sever...

"Why the long face, chil'?" Saggy Jean asked. "What've you done?"

Shut up, woman. Leave me be.

The others did not come to my defense. They had

stopped protecting me months ago. They didn't know why, but they knew I'd gone sour. Could have been the grey in my skin, the recession of my gums, the red in my eyes...

My fingers worried the stained, frayed hair of the doll in my lap, a reminder of innocence lost, of ridiculous totems of nurturing and play. Mine, but without meaning now. Without joy.

"I've done nothing," I spat at Saggy Jean, spraying the words at the others as well.

"Careful, chil'," Saggy Jean said, her green eyes taunting me. "We let you crash here, give you food and such. We could easily move you along, out to the world to fend for yourself. Though I suspect the world should be more scared of you than you of it."

I WAS TIRED. I wanted my garden.

I left the brood at the Shitty Shanty town and made my way to my garden to rest. I longed for my face in the dirt, nothing but the stars and the petals in my view. I looked back over my shoulder to make sure Snoopy Saggy Jean had her ass firmly set in place, with no intentions of disturbing me, but she was not there.

When did she leave? I didn't notice her go?

My step hastened and chest tightened. By the time I

reached my dirt haven I was at a full run, panting over a dry tongue.

And there she was.

In *my* garden.

Her arms buried in *my* dirt.

She looked at me, streaks of tears marring her wrinkled old face.

"You've been busy," she said, her lip trembling.

Rib cages, unearthed by Saggy Jean's prying hands, framing crops and bushels of all manner of flora; my natural planters for the rebirth of tainted life.

"I count twelve, girl. Though tha's no surprise, I 'pose. Known for a while, I have."

Her hands sifted through the dirt and meat, the flesh fertilizer.

"They have transformed," I said. "Grown purity and beauty out of the ruined, tainted creation."

"We are all ruined in our own way," Saggy said. "The fixin' ain't up to you. You are a murderous beast."

"I am an angel," I said.

"Of death," she said.

"Of life," I said.

"You are evil."

"I took her to fix this. She is finally useful," I said.

Saggy Jean stilled and moved to me, remaining on her knees. A tall woman when she straightened her spine, she moved in front of my face, forcing eye contact.

"Took who?" she asked.

I paused.

She's baiting me.

I should not have given in to her taunting, to her challenge. But I did. I was proud, and I wanted to boast.

"I took Taissa, of course, while she slept. While her parents lay sleeping meters from her room, dwelling on money, on their fading looks, on their stunted attempts at coitus. And she was silent when I took her. In fact, I think I saw a smile dance across those soft, pink lips."

Saggy Jean looked into my eyes and saw the red fires of hell.

But she did not look away.

"You are not the first I have encountered, beast. This is old hat for me."

She reached out and took my hands in hers, and pulled me close.

"Oh you poor, tortured things. May you be at peace. Both of you."

She pulled my hands to her lips and licked my fingertips with her pasty, meaty tongue. I pushed away, falling back to the dirt and scrambling deep into the safety of my garden. Saggy Jean's belly rumbled as laughter brewed and boiled inside her, finding its release in hearty cackles as she walked away, leaving me splayed out in the dirt.

"Hands against the wall," the burly officer barked.

Saggy Jean, Rita, Wilber, and the rest of the leavings of human dignity bellied up against the wall, trembling and mewling like battered livestock. The police tossed the entire underbelly of the shanty town, dredging up garbage and cans and meager belongings worth less than the shit on the soles of their boots. Except for in Saggy Jean's tent.

"Who lives here?" the officer said, poking Saggy's tent with a billy stick.

Saggy raised a trembling hand.

After a brief, hushed discussion, an officer adorned Saggy with the silver bracelets, dragging her to the cruiser with her hands wrenched behind her back. As the officer shoved her head down and pushed her into the back seat, she looked up. Looked for me. When her eyes met mine, I smiled and held out the cellphone in my hand.

"... an anonymous tip," one officer said to another. "She's got the weapons stashed in here. And blood-soaked fucking everything..."

Then something happened. Something horrible. She smiled at me and nodded.

Everything around me slowed, and the sound muffled to a warbled womb in my ears. I felt woozy, watching the CSI's cordon off the camp with their bright yellow tape, moving to and fro around Saggy Jean's tent, carrying off contents like worker ants on a mission for their queen. The weapons I planted, the clothes, the blood.

The jars.

The jars?

Two, five, eight, I lost count... jars with eyes, liquids, herbs and powders. Talismans and feathers, orbs and scrolls.

"Fuck me," an officer said. "Fucking witchcraft. Figured it was something warped like that. Not looking forward to finding those bodies."

I slipped away, away from the locusts of the crime scene, away from the eyes of my neighbours, and away from Saggy Jean's cackle seeping out the window of the police cruiser. And I ran. I ran up the slope and across the road and to my precious, beloved garden of rebirth.

And I breathed a sigh of relief.

My flowers were still there.

My greenery was still there.

The stars still shone, dazzling their sparkling light off the dew of my petals.

But something wasn't right.

Movement, minute and delicate, surging through the flora like subtle sea waves. I dropped to my knees and moved closer, examining the petals of my beloveds. The plants, the greenery and the colourful flora, were crawling with borers and aphids, whiteflies and mealybugs, consuming the growth and spreading bacterial mold and rot along their paths. My chest tightened, and a scream erupted from my throat. I fumbled at the soft flesh of the petals, trying desperately to brush off the invaders, but insects flowed from beneath my fingernails, eating everything in their wake. And the world became loud, Saggy Jean's voice booming in my head.

All you touch will die. All her delicate fingers touch will be consumed by the hatred in you, beast. Leave the girl. She is useless to you now.

Floating. Flying. Limbo.

Taissa's body slumped to the ground, her throaty screams reducing to feminine shrieks as officers descended upon her, comforting her and attempting to quell her panic. From above and around and below I watched as Taissa scrambled to remember where she was, who she was, what she was as the garden around her wilted into death.

A WISH

*W*armth, wet and gritty, pooled beneath my fluttering eyelids. I opened my eyes, and the heat flowed out, trickling down my cheeks and soaking my shirt. I grazed the dampness with my fingertips, then held my hand in front of my face. Shimmering crimson stained the tips of my pallid fingers, the same red wetness that saturated the front of my shirt. My vision was cloudy, a combined product of head trauma and blood flowing over my face. I wiped my eyes with the back of my hand and gave a few ferocious blinks to clean away the mental and physical haze. Time to assess the situation.

The front of the car was akin to a crumpled accordion, wrapped around an oak tree at the bottom of the ravine. I was still buckled into my seat. The driver's side seatbelt was hanging in place, neglected at a time when it had been needed most. My husband was always obstinate when it came to things he didn't prefer, one of which was wearing a seatbelt when the new laws came into effect. No harm no foul for decades.

Until tonight.

A stone's throw from the car, beyond a gaping chasm in the windshield, the bottoms of his cheap loafers were staring me in the face from the forest bed.

I released my seatbelt and opened my door. It took a great deal of wriggling and contorting to get out; my knees had become intimately and forcefully acquainted with the dash. Once I had struggled free, I stood wavering on tentative legs, legs I wasn't sure would hold me up let alone carry me very far. But they did, and I floated along on autopilot to what was left of my husband. He was dead. Very dead. Mangled, ended abruptly with such violence and force that he was no longer recognizable in the pile of inanimate meat that lay before me. This is what I'd hoped for time and time again throughout our marriage, but I hadn't imagined it would be so terrible. Reality sank in and panicked sobs erupted from my chest. I needed help. I wasn't hurt—not badly anyways—but I needed someone. I ran into the woods, in no direction in particular, hoping to eventually intersect a road, a house, a person, anything.

The darkness of the midnight hour was compounded by the heavy canopy of tree branches combating the glow of the moon, making an already treacherous and foreign environment even less navigable. The trail was disjointed, speckled with broken lunar illumination. I followed the most even ground I could find, stopping to gather myself each time I came to a clearing or an opening in the claustrophobic fauna. Every step I took brought me farther along the path that wasn't a path, and deeper into lost.

My mind needed to slow down, to process what had just happened, and the silence and solitude of the night woods the perfect place for reflection. A car accident. My husband was killed. Those were the plain facts. That should have been troubling enough, but no. What corroded my heart and nerves was the internal dialogue that had transpired within my bitter and tired mind just prior to our sedan plummeting down that slope. We had fought, as we typically did after a shindig where booze flowed like water, but my mind was fighting a battle cumulative of all the combat we had engaged in during our long decade of marriage. All the hurt, the disrespect, the mundane squabbles. I had decided at that moment, in that car careening towards our doom, that I hated my husband. I wished, a whisper in my mind, that he would just die. And die he did.

Now there I was, wandering in the middle of nowhere, heading deep into the woods to God knows what end. But it felt right, and I craved something that felt good. As I passed through trees and bushes, the branches and tendrils of leaves and vines groped at me with their coarse fingers, snagging my hair and clothes like hungry predators. Panic set in as I grew overwhelmed by the tactile assault. I closed my eyes, blindly thrashing forwards until the forest wall gave way to a clearing, and I plummeted into the moss.

It was an odd clearing, out of place and unnatural. Set in the center was a stone cabin, warm light flickering in the foggy windows, a plume of smoke coughing gently from the brick chimney. Relief washed over me, and I stumbled up to my feet, anxious for consolation from another soul, but quickly retracted my trajectory towards solace. At first blush, the cabin had looked quaint and cozy, a veritable cliché of an innocuous hideaway off the beaten path. Now that I eyeballed it with more scrutiny, I found that the little haven had some eerie quirks, sideways enough for my mind to raise the red flags.

The windows, flickering with what seemed to be the glow from an active fire, were stained a yellowish-red, as if fluid had been splashed on them and left to dry. Amulets and talismans of all sorts hung from the gutter, dangling and clanking against each other in the breeze. The pathways were lined by off-white decor which, upon further inspection, appeared to be bones. I was about to retreat and find another destination to conclude my wandering, when a crack rang out behind me, resonating off the surfaces of the forest.

I turned and saw them. They saw me—likely they had seen me all along—but I finally saw them. My gut had been shouting at me that I hadn't been alone during my short travels, but I now had solid confirmation. There, walking towards me, hip to hip, were row upon row of all manner of unearthly creatures the likes of which I couldn't conjure up even in my most feverish nightmares. Jaws hanging haphazardly, skin torn and battered, limbs missing or otherwise rearranged. They were a sight to behold, so much so that I had to suppress projectile vomit from spewing forth from my gob. I turned back to the cabin and saw more monstrosities ambling towards the building. If I didn't know better—not that I knew what was going on at all—I would have thought they were forming a line. They didn't seem interested in me at all. Regardless, I felt the urge to scream and run, until a cracking voice broke through the groans and grinding of the march of the dead.

"A right mess, and a fresh one at that," the voice said.

I looked to the stoop, and found what I presumed to be the cabin's owner standing on the porch, leaning on the rail and surveying the mass of macabre before him. His hair was long but tidy, gathered in a wispy, white bun. His eyes were gold and his skin grey, the grooves and divots on his face suggesting he was many miles from youth. He extended a long finger and curled it to beckon me.

"You."

I went without hesitation. If I strolled by him on the street, I would cringe at his aesthetic, but out in the woods, on that porch, he looked like a butterfly among cockroaches. I dashed to the cabin, traversing the stairs in a single bound, and stood in front of the door. I grimaced as the monsters continued storming the cabin in slow motion, but the curator seemed cool as a cucumber, so my mood followed suit. I looked at the door, and saw a brass nameplate bolted to the heavy wood, engraved with a simple title:

The Translator

The man swung the door open and stepped to the side, motioning me through with an open palm. I obliged. Once inside, I looked around and was pleased to find an average little dwelling furnished with floral couches, doilies, and ceramic ornaments one would expect in the abode of any octogenarian. There were pictures of scenery and geese on the walls, and a fresh pot of tea boiling on the wood stove. Perhaps I would find comfort here after all.

"No," he said sharply. "This is where I live, not where I work. We conduct our business downstairs."

Before I had time to question him, he spun around on his calloused feet and headed to the back of the kitchen, opening what I imagined was a door to the basement. I was in no state to argue, so I followed. Besides, deeper into the cabin meant further from those creatures outside. Unfortunately, the basement was what basements are; damp, dark, and terrifying. It was a single room lit by sparse candle light, the walls decorated with a hoarder's share of knick-knacks, trinkets, and personal effects. I imaged the hundreds, possibly thousands of people attached to these items.

"So, love, tell me your story."

I tried, I really did. I felt the muscles in my diaphragm

expand and contract, and air propel out of my mouth, but the only sound I produced was a guttural growl that sounded like a grizzly bear in heat. Startled, my hands flew over my mouth.

"It's a bit off-putting at first," he laughed. "To you, that is. Doesn't bother me one bit, so don't fret over that. I'm no stranger to your language."

I cocked my head at him, puzzled.

"The din of the dead, lovey. Once you're gone, you all speak the same language, and use the same tones. No matter what corner of this spinning rock you're from, you're all the same after the end."

I'm dead?

Those were the words I spoke in my mind, but it came out as a god awful, sputtering garble. No matter. He understood.

"Yes," he said, kneeling in front of me and taking my hands in his. "I'm so sorry. No one comes here if they make it out alive. I don't exist in the flesh world."

But... why? How?

"There's no time to get into logistics, sweetheart. You were lucky enough to make it to me, but time is short. We must do this soon, or you'll be cast out with the rest of the tardy to wander these woods eternally. If you are late arriving here, I cannot help."

What?

"This is a transitional place—the lounge of the afterlife if you will—and those who are lucky enough to win this lottery get one final wish before carrying on to their final destination. Or returning to their life. There is no rhyme or reason behind who gets this opportunity. You are selected randomly, so don't go thinking your high or low levels of morality earned you a spot past my doorstep. It's a crap shoot, and you came out on top."

A wish?

"Yes, you get one wish; one last kick at the cat before it's all final. But there's a catch. It's not just a simple wish like the ones granted by my brethren summoned from lamps. No, is a limit to the wished I grant. Your wish is a word.

A word?

"Yes, a word. You will wish to speak one word, at any time, in any place, from anyone, and I will make that happen. Only one word. You have but five minutes to consider, then you must tell me your word. I will translate it for you, through the speech of whomever you choose, at whatever time you choose. If you are clever, you might alter the course of your life, or your death. Choose poorly, and you've wasted our breath."

A daunting task, one muddled by having to simultaneously grapple with the knowledge that my life had been thrust into limbo. One word. What could change things? I could say something to get my husband to summon a taxi home from the party, then the crash would never occur. But how could I be sure one word would make that happen? I couldn't. Perhaps a word of warning, before the car loses control? Perhaps something to ensure that I drove?

"Time is ticking," he said, looking at his watch.

My life spun a manic reel in my mind. One word, to anyone, from anyone. So much power, so little time. I wanted to live, but had my life even been worth living? Could I possibly change more than my moment of death, perhaps the course of my life?

Then I knew. Instantly and conclusively.

I breathed my wish to him in my newfound voice, my din of the damned.

He raised a bushy eyebrow, then shrugged his shoulders.

"Creative, I'll give you that," he said. "Cold, but clever. Very well."

He yanked off my necklace and mumbled some incantation while worrying it through his fingers. I looked at the paraphernalia cluttering his walls and understood what it was. I was one of many who had been granted a wish. A word.

In a flash I was somewhere else, watching a scene unfold though my spot in the unspecified dimension which I occupied. My mother- and father-in-law, many moons ago, two young adults slamming into each other on a busy sidewalk. They gathered up their spilled belongings, then stood and looked deep into each other's eyes. After a few minutes of benign chit chat, he asked his question.

"Hey, I'm only in town for one day on business. Wanna catch a flick? Or a coffee, maybe?"

She looked at him with lust in her eyes and parted her full lips.

"No." She looked shocked and confused as the word moved over her tongue and out into the air.

He scowled at her, stung by the word, and disappeared into the crowd.

FREED

The song rang out, a jovial melody from the rickety old player piano in the corner. The notes were warbled and out of tune, but toes were tapping just the same. An inebriated blacksmith was stomping the floor in a feeble attempt at a jittery jig, the clomp of his boot rattling the glasses hanging above the bar.

The Rusty Rim was hopping and rowdy. The train had rolled in early that morning for its monthly trip, bringing with it a fresh crop of wares and liquor and weapons to rile everyone up right fine. The day had been full of buying and selling, testing and using, and now everyone and their dog was crammed into Plummer Creek's sole saloon to marinate their excitement in the new shipment of top-shelf liquor from above the border. Lads from up north came to whet their whistles and sate their aching loins with the ladies that made the upper floor of the Rusty Rim their home and business.

All was well. People laughed and shouted, glasses were clinked together, playing cards snapped against the freshly polished wood of the old bar tables as some cowboy cleaned up another round of cards. A wispy whore stumbled up the stairs on her two-inch heels, leading a chubby trick in mustache up the stairs by his boner, wet already seeping through the front of his slacks.

Big Sammy Purdue stood sentry at the back wall, leaning against a post and watching his town as they drank and fucked their way to stupidity. Laughter and smoke hung heavy in the air, accented by the twang of the player piano and the muffled humping from above.

It was the wee hours of the morning, and neither towns-folk nor visitors showed any signs of slowing. Sammy sat on a bar stool and tipped his hat over his eyes, resigned to perform his duty of monitoring the biped livestock. His eyes grew heavy and dropped to the floor, attempting to sneak in a waking rest.

The creak and slap of the swinging saloon doors drew his attention.

The hour was late, and though the party was hours from being complete, late-comers were a rarity. If anyone had not been in that saloon by 10 pm, they were either old and feeble, or suckling at their mama's teat. And even some of those babes were in that bar, their mouths over one nipple while a stranger's hand occupied the other.

But there she was, strutting through that door hours after the town had cleared the streets, coming from God knows where with nary a business or home open and welcoming, other than the Rusty Rim.

She was stunning. Long ginger braid flowing down her back, ivory white skin kissed with a dusting of gentle freckles, coral lips plump and moist. She was tall, pert near taller than any woman in town, Sammy reckoned, though he couldn't see the height of heels she wore beneath her baby-blue skirts. Regardless, her presence was commanding and startling, a fire raging in those sultry emerald eyes.

She saw him. Her eyes locked onto his and he froze. She did too, for a moment, then a smile quivered on the corner of her lip. He tipped his hat with a shaky hand, and she curtsied to return the greeting. When she turned her attention to the bar, striding across that miserable, sticky floor in long, graceful strides, Big Sammy heaved out a sigh of relief.

She approached the bar, and he watched her lips move, naming her poison to the smirking barkeep who couldn't keep his eyes above the line of her corset. She leaned against the damp wood as he poured, amber liquor splashing from the glass as his hand shook. She took the glass from him and pressed it to her lips, pouring the burning liquid over her tongue.

Big Sammy swallowed hard, the unfamiliar swell in his

trousers causing his cheeks to flush. He sat on the nearest barstool and crossed his legs.

She moved through the room, dodging the drunk and disorderly, swaying around tables and the piano, surveying the crowd as if she was selecting a fine cut of meat.

And she settled on the finest.

Paulie, the mayor's son, hair and eyes as black as his soul, hand firmly clenched on a young whore's bosom. She flinched, her barely pubescent body surely tender and unaccustomed to such abuse, her lips forced into a smile that deceived itself with a glaring tremor. Paulie threw his head back and roared out a laugh, a horrible sound fueled by excessive amounts of whiskey and heavy red meat stolen straight from the taxpayers' pockets. The girl started to cry.

"What's the matter, young cunt? " Paulie slurred, his hand slipping off her breast and jamming between her legs as she yelped. "Anxious to have it?"

The men around the table laughed, nervous but amused.

The beautiful stranger laughed the loudest. "I suspect she's anxious, yes, but to have that ten seconds of her life over and done with so she can move onto more pleasurable activities. Like cleaning the vomit out of the men's latrine."

Her voice was honey, dripping from those coral lips, cool and sweet and soothing. But her words matched the fire in her eyes, scathing, feral, roaring.

Paulie raised his eyes to the newcomer and released his grasp on the young girl.

"And what have we here?" he said, hauling his mass out of the chair and wobbling towards the ginger angel. "A fresh cut of meat, I see."

The din of voices and clinks dampened, leaving only the tinking and tonking of the player piano piercing the tension in the air. Paulie wobbled towards the new woman, one hand on his crotch, the other reaching for the front of her skirt. Big Sammy tucked his hand under his vest, resting his thumb and forefinger on his Colt.

He didn't need to.

She didn't need his protection.

Paulie's fingers brushed the lace on the front of her skirt at the same time as her hand brushed his throat, her sharpened nails digging, piercing, then tearing out his trachea. She held the severed organ in front of his face before bringing it to her own, catching a drop of dripping blood on the tip of her soft, pink tongue.

"HolyJesusFuckingChrist," Sammy breathed out.

The saloon was still and silent, save that fucking player piano, whose every note shattered the remaining nerves in the room. After a moment of processing, the screaming and trampling began, some lunging for the exit, other craning and rushing to see better the carnage that had come to visit their sedate little town.

The Madame rushed her girls up the stairs, slamming into Big Sammy on the way by. Big Sammy came to, jostled into action. He walked over to the woman, gun in hand.

"Ma'am," he said, instinctively tipping his hat.

"Good sir," she said, her voice moist velvet.

"You know, we frown upon murder 'round these parts".

"They do in most parts, I'm sure."

"Indeed."

She looked into Big Sammy's eyes, Paulie's trachea still swinging in the air in front of her face, her fingertips teasing the tendons and muscles.

"I don't suppose you know who this is?" Big Sammy asked, focusing on the emeralds embedded in her blood-stained face.

"Was," she said, with a wink and a giggle.

"What?"

"Who he *was*," she repeated, innocent humour in her voice.

"Uh huh," he said, resisting the urge to smile. "Well then, yes, do you know who that *was*?"

"A piece of shit," she said, averting her eyes and looking down at the throat-less body slumped on the floor.

"Yes, well, be that as it may," Big Sammy paused, shoving his distaste for Paulie to the back of his mind, "he is—was, the Mayor's son. Mayor Bill ain't gonna take none too kindly to that."

"Huh," she said, looking back up into Sammy's eyes. "I suppose the Mayor didn't take kind to his son being scolded at all. 'Splains why he can carry on the way he does, like an animal in heat."

"I gotta take you in, Ma'am."

She gave the slightest nod, a red curl loosing itself from her bun and cascading over the milky skin on her chest. Big Sammy cringed at the dichotomy of vomit rising along with his erection as she dropped her piece of Paulie's throat. It landed on her feet with a splut, and slid off onto the floor, leaving a smear across her lily-white skin. She raised her head and looked back into Big Sammy's eyes, her plump lashes fluttering over those sparkling greens.

"Shall we?" she said.

"Unfortunately we shall," Big Sammy said.

He rattled in his boots as she stepped forward and slid her slender hand through his arm. He cleared his throat, and they walked out of the saloon, arm in arm, like a couple off to a night at the theater.

"She looks cold."

"She fine," Big Sammy said, looking down his nose at the young deputy shivering behind the desk. "She ain't cold. Cool as a cucumber, but beneath that pretty mask, she's on fire."

The woman sat behind heavy iron bars, legs crossed, foot tapping along to a silent tune. She quietly picked away at her fingernails, chipping away the blood that had dried along her cuticles.

"When can we go?" the young deputy asked, his boot

tapping a frantic staccato under the desk. "How long we gotta keep her here?"

"Son?"

"Yessir?"

"Go on home, now."

"But who will guard—"

"I'll guard her."

"But—"

"I will guard her," Big Sammy said, grasping the young man's shoulder in his firm hand.

The young deputy didn't question it further. He sprang from his chair, knocking over a mug of coffee in the process, and barely pausing before turning tail and running out the door. He didn't question why the sheriff, who had more important political duties, would sit in the town jail guarding a prisoner, and a woman at that.

"But you ain't no woman, is ya?"

"Pardon?" she said, looking up from her manicure.

"Nothin'."

He watched her, the rhythm of her foot, the curve of her hip, her hair moving in the wind seeking in the window at the ceiling.

She was a beautiful monster.

"Name?"

"Pardon?" she said.

"You heard me," he said, still staring, still standing.

"Ain't got one."

"Bullshit."

"That ain't it, fer sure."

He grabbed the chair from behind the desk and sauntered over to the bars of her cage. He set the chair down in front of the cell, hiked up his pants, and sat, crossing his legs in kind.

"What do you want?"

"Pardon?"

Big Sammy sighed.

"Nothing wrong with your hearing, ma'am."

"There sure isn't."

"Jus' your compliance."

"No sir," she said, uncrossing her legs and folding her hands in her lap. "I mean no trouble."

"No trouble? The mayor's son might disagree, if he could voice his concerns."

She snickered. "Suppose he would. Well, no trouble, 'cept for him."

"Why him?"

"That poor girl—"

"No," Big Sammy said firmly. "I watched you."

She looked up, her eyes large and still. "I know you did."

"I watched you case the saloon, seeing everyone, looking at everyone and for someone. You found him."

She said nothing, just stared back.

"Who hired you?"

"No one," she said, sitting back and crossing her legs.

"The mayor has plenty of enemies. No better way to get to him than his only spawn."

"I should be expecting some thanks, then, it would seem."

"But who did this?"

"I did. You were there."

Big Sammy sighed again. He leaned forward. "Ma'am, look. Someone sent you, I know. A pretty creature such as yourself doesn't suit this kind of business. Help me out here, so I can help you."

He looked at her, and she looked at him. Into him. Her eyes gleamed with wetness, her lip twitched ever so slightly.

"Help me?" she said, a slight quaver in her voice. "I killed a man, sir."

Big Sammy had nothing to say. This woman, who had appeared in town cocksure and strong, crumbled into her own lap, wracking sobs convulsing her body.

She's so young, he thought, looking at her thick hair, her porcelain skin. *Who did this to her?*

"Who made you do this?" Big Sammy said, reaching for his belt.

She couldn't speak, only despair poured out.

He knew better.

But he didn't care.

He pulled out the iron key ring and walked over to the jailhouse door. A quick look out the window, then he locked them inside. When he turned, she was sitting up, hands trembling, face glistening with tears.

The sound of the key in the lock made her shoulders lurch and his stomach lunge into his throat. The door swung open with a blood-curdling screech. He took one feeble step, then stood there, the tip of his boots just slightly over the line into the cell, submerged in a skiff of hay. She stayed on the bench, chest heaved out from breath held in her lungs, tears frozen in her eyes.

He inhaled deeply, the smell of the hay, the scent of the fragrance on her hair and her skin; she was an intoxicating cocktail. He stepped forward and sat on the opposite end of the bench.

"Have you heard of our laws, ma'am?"

She paused. Her honesty took its time, but it came. "Y-yes."

"You know what we do to murderers."

Another pause.

"Ma'am?"

"Yes. I do," she said, the quaver returning.

"You knew you would die, pulling a stunt like that."

"I did, yes," she said. A single, solid nod told him what he wanted to know.

"You want to die."

"Yes."

"But why?"

She paused, seemingly counting the straws of hay at her feet, then looked up at him with resolve.

"I got nowhere and nothin'," she declared, wiping a stray

tear from her eye. "I have nothin' in the world, and no where I care to get it. I'm done with bein', but don't have no interest in the endin' part."

She looked confident, now. She was dead set on her fate; scared, but prepared.

So young, he thought again. He looked at her face, flawless, her eyes clear and bright, her body lean and long and curved. *A beautiful waste.*

"Will it hurt?" she asked, tears forming against her battle for composure.

He nodded.

"The Mayor has taken none too kindly to the loss of his boy. You're to be hung in the woods, left for the wolves, I'm afraid."

"Hrmph," she said, grimacing. "Sounds messy."

"Will be, but you won't know."

She shivered and clasped her shoulders.

So slender, so delicate.

Without thinking, actively pushing reason aside, Big Sammy slid up next to her on that bench and wrapped his thick arm around her. She melted into him, resting her head on his chest and letting the tears flow.

"When does my time end?"

"Tonight," Big Sammy said. "After dark."

She sat back and put her hand on his face.

"Will you be there? For me?"

He wanted to say yes. He wanted to tell her that everything would be okay, that he would save her and take her away and give her what she was missing.

He said nothing. He leaned forward and pressed his lips against hers. She startled, gently pulling away for the briefest of moments, then leaned into his kiss, pushing her mouth hard onto his, slipping her tongue between his teeth and rolling it around his mouth.

The cell was dusty and hazy, the high noon sun streaming through the windows at the ceiling. Big Sammy thought that she was the most beautiful thing he had ever seen. His hands were clumsy, frantic, as he yanked at the soft blue ribbon, pulling away the boned corset from her delicate body. She ripped and shed as well, freeing herself of layers of silk and crinoline until she stood there in the light, sun shimmering off her pale flesh, nipples dark and erect, and a glimmering sheen between her legs.

He took her. On the bench, in the hay, against the wall. She cried and she came, and he moved frantically inside her until he felt his entire body might explode, the force of his pleasure and her pleasure stealing the very marrow from his bones. He fell to his knees, spasms of release echoing through his body so intense it bordered pain.

"Dear fuck," he moaned, rocking back and forth on his knees.

It seemed to go on forever, the pulsing, the bursting ache, the euphoria. When he finally came down, his cock diminished, sated, quenched, he looked up.

And his stomach dropped into his bowels.

She was sitting on the bench, legs crossed, picking at blood on her cuticles.

Blood.

So much blood.

He looked down at his wilted member. His torso and groin were drenched in blood, his cock looking like it had been dipped in a freshly slain corpse.

It was as if the wind had been knocked out of him. He examined himself, verifying that his package was completely there and intact. The blood wasn't his, he determined, but why...

He scrambled to his feet, scooping his trousers and shirt off the floor before backing out of the cell and slamming the lock closed. He poured his mug of coffee over himself, swatting away the blood and grime. He wiped away what he could with a nearby bandana, then squirmed into his wet clothes.

He caught his breath, dug deep for his last nerve, and looked into the cell.

There she sat, coy smile plastered across her face, her thighs covered in a thick coat of blood. Her skin glowed white against the dark crimson that dripped out on the floor beneath her.

Beast, he thought, as he unlocked the jail door and let sunlight join them in that musty room.

"WALK FASTER."

Mayor Bill jammed the barrel of his rifle into the woman's ribs. She buckled, but continued walking. No faster, though, Big Sammy noticed.

They had been going at a fair clip, the darkness of the night and the groping claws of the forest putting some fuel in their step. The pit was a good kilometer straight into the brush, single-track trail leading the way through the branches and brambles. Two green deputies led the way, three sheets to the wind. Big Sammy led the woman by the arm, with Mayor Bill close on their heels. Behind, two more seasoned deputies trailed, watching to ensure everyone was where and how they were supposed to be.

She did not falter, Big Sammy thought as he watched her pink feet, slender and graceful, the toes of a dancer. She did not stumble as the briars and the pinecones pierced her flesh, and the rocks bruised the underbelly of her arches. And though her face was contained under a burlap hood, he knew she was smiling. He could feel it.

Big Sammy shivered. He always hated these late-night promenades into the woods. It was dark and quiet, but not quiet enough. Twigs cracked in the deep of the woods, far beyond the fall of their boots. The deeper they went, the darker it got, not even the moonlight dared to join them on their journey.

The clearing exploded upon them like a gulp of air, a reprieve from the claustrophobic clench of the dense woods.

The hanging platform stood sentry in the middle, the wood weathered and rotting, its weathered, bloodstained noose swaying in the breeze.

"Okay, darlin'," Big Sammy said, leading her by the arm up the crooked steps, one, two, three. He paused after he had positioned her in front of the noose, square in the middle of the drop panel. He skin, almost glowing white in the darkness, drew his eye to her bosom, barely moving under her soft breath. He moved closer and wrapped the noose around the sack. Her smell was intoxicating, delicious...

"Big Sammy," the Mayor said, his face red and breathing hard. "I ain't satisfied with this. Not one bit."

"Bill, she won't pose no problems. Let's just get this done."

"Too easy!" Bill shouted, his hat rattling around on top of his fat, bald head. "She be gettin' off with this too fucking clean!"

"She's paying for her crime with her life. No greater punishment. Shooting her would do the job, but that's quicker—"

"Worse," Bill said. "A bullet would snuff her instantly. Even a few minute hang is too quick for the likes of her."

"What, then?" Big Sammy said, looking at the raging man with revenge in his eyes.

Mayor Bill looked over his shoulder at the muscle standing behind him, two large deputies with more beef than brain. They were his personal guard, mongrels that trailed

him everywhere. At Bill's nod, they stepped up on the platform and shouldered Big Sammy to the side.

"What's all this, then?" Big Sammy said, clopping down
the steps and face-to-face with Mayor Bill.

"This is the punishment yer too yellow to serve," Bill said.

"Bill, the laws are clear—"

"The laws are soft! You're soft!"

Were it up to Mayor Bill, even the orphans that stole a
bite of biscuit would be scalped in front of the whole town.
The mayor had a thirst for violence, and a penchant for over-
reactive rage. And he had a great fondness for the manhan-
dling of women, a trait which he had passed on to his dearly
departed son.

She was a murderer. A monster, perhaps. But Big Sammy
cringed at the thought of what Bill might have in store for her.

The thug with the single brow that spanned from ear to
ear, ripped the hood from the woman's head. Her face was a
blank slate of emotions, but Big Sammy thought he saw the
tail end of a waning smirk.

"You rancid cunt," the thug said, his breath pushing into
her mouth.

"Up she goes, boys," Mayor Bill said, clapping his hands.

He was no longer angry. He was smiling. Excited.

The thug grabbed her by the shoulders, and his partner
crouched and wrapped his arm around her legs. In a fluid
spin that would have impressed the Ringling brothers, she
was upside down, her slender ankles threaded through the

noose. A few pulls and loops later, and she hung inverted through the noose by her ankles. Her dress and petticoat fell over her face as she swung.

"Off with that mess," Bill said, rubbing his hands together.

A few swipes from a few knives and her dress, petticoat, and undergarments were in shreds, clasped in the hands of the Brothers Gross. The egghead without the voice sniffed her panties, then stuck them in the pocket of his vest. The brothers stepped off the platform and joined the other deputies at Bill's side.

"Now hold up," Big Sammy said, raising his hand and sauntering over to Bill. The brothers stepped forward and Sammy stopped. "What's your plan?"

"Justice, Deputy," Bill said, a smirk on his fat face. "Pleasurable justice."

Bill took a step towards the platform. Big Sammy allowed it, but did not stand down.

"Girl," Bill said as he stepped up the stairs, one, two, three. "That was my son, you know."

"I know," she said, her voice full of sugar and calm.

"You know, do you?" Bill laughed, looking incredulously at the four deputies and Big Sammy, then back at the woman. "You knew, but you did it anyways? How d'you think I'd feel about that, you stealin' my son from me?"

"Angry. Full of Rage."

Bill walked up to her, his face mere centimeters from her

naked body. He pursed his lips and blew on her navel, bending and drawing a line of hot air down her stomach and between her ample breasts until he was looking in her eyes.

"Anger?" he said. "Rage? Understatements, my dear."

She looked at him, and her face stretched, the widest smile Big Sammy thought he had ever seen.

"Good," she said.

She swung forward ever so slightly and thrust her tongue into Mayor's Bill mouth. He spat her out, and she laughed, a braying cackle that vibrated against the night.

Mayor Bill was no longer full of perverse humour.

He sputtered, gagging on his own thoughts until he could spew them out.

"Enough!"

The gleam of the Bowie knife sparkled in her green eyes as Mayor Bill pulled it from the sheath on his hip. Big Sammy started yelling and running, but the brothers had latched onto his arms, wrapped a leg around each of his, and pushed into his hips, locking him in place.

Mayor Bill yelled out as he raised his arm, spittle flying from his mouth onto her beautiful flesh. The blade went through her like butter, the tip making its entrance at the hairline between her legs, delving hilt deep by the time it reached her bellybutton. Bill sawed and heaved, pulling and pushing the blade until it was firmly jammed against her breast bone. He stumbled off the platform and fell to his knees.

The woods fell silent. The men did not speak, barely

breathing, and the wildlife had hushed into stunned silence. Big Sammy's jaw was slack, quiet tears streaming down his face as the world around him paused to process what had just happened.

The woman hung there by her ankles, her tender body glistening in the cool night air. The blood was so dark against the white of her flesh. Her organs looked black in the meager illumination, spilling out of her like a butcher's leavings, landing in plips and plops on the platform below. Her hair, warm strawberry ringlets, waved to and fro through the puddle of meat and blood.

She was smiling. Blood poured down her face, over her eyes and into her mouth. And she continued to smile.

Bill laughed. A fat, clubbed finger came up, pointing at her naked and split body, and he laughed, a gruesome hee-haw that awakened the night. Crows heckled, frogs sang, and wolves howled in the distance.

Nothing could be done for her. Her insides were on the outside, draped over her breasts, face, and shoulders like thick, meaty streamers, the pool of blood and organs spanning the entire platform and dripping to the dirt below. The brothers, realizing it was done, released Big Sammy and went to Bill's side.

Big Sammy jumped up to the platform, bypassing the stairs and crawling up on top, sliding through blood and gore to reach the woman. He gave her shoulders a shake, expecting nothing but hoping for something, anything, but was greeted with a limp, dripping carcass. He gathered her red locks in his hands and brought them to his face, trying to smell the fragrance of magnolia hidden beneath the stench of copper and bile.

Big Sammy cried. Out of shock, horror, disgust. He loved her, but she was a monster, and it was all so terrible. The displaced trachea, the bloody coitus, the savage disembowelment. Behind him he could hear the deputies and the mayor, guffawing and pounding each other on the back with congratulatory slaps.

It enraged Big Sammy. He was angry at them, at the inhumanity, at the men they were and the world that accepted them as such. Big Sammy braced himself in the slick pool of blood and stood. His boots slipped out from under him, and he came splashing down on his back in a puddle of the woman's organ and fluids. The men below erupted into raucous laughter, snorts and whistles and whooping and hollering enough to wake the dead. Big Sammy closed his eyes and tried to calm the storm swelling in his chest. He breathed, in and out, focusing on the sound of his own heart.

And a gurgle.

He opened his eyes.

A hiss.

He looked up at the mass of hair hanging above him, swaying gently in the breeze.

Swaying too much.

The laughter continued, but all Big Sammy could hear

was the gurgling and muffled belching from the organs around him, slithering and gyrating in the slick of blood. He reached up and grabbed the mass of red tresses and parted it to the side, revealing a face white and wide as the moon.

She was smiling, impossibly large, rows of teeth sprouted from bloody gums, protruding though her cheeks and piercing the flesh on her face and her very own eyes. She twisted her neck clear around until it was contorted in a spiral, and reached into herself with newly sprouted talons. Muscles popped from her biceps as she tore herself completely in two, wriggling her feet until both halves dropped from the noose and landed with a dull splut on the bloody platform beside Big Sammy.

The laughter stopped. The din from the forest had quieted as well, the creatures making their escape long before the men had realized anything had gone awry. The knuckle-draggers that called themselves deputies stepped back as the Mayor froze, trembling on the ground.

"What... the... fu—"

One half of the woman wriggled to life, razor sharp legs sprouting from the ball of her foot up her buttock and all the way to the back of her neck. Thousands of legs sprouted on every square centimeter of her surface like black fingers hungry for contact, quivering and feeling the surrounding air. Despite her insectoid form, her face remained relatively intact, though only a half. And that smile split her face right to her ear.

Once that half had fully formed, the second half wriggled to life, attaching itself to the end of the first, becoming a twelve-foot long, thick, meaty millipede of murder.

Big Sammy knew he was screaming. He could feel the strain in his belly and the force of air passing over his tongue. He could feel his bladder give way, soaking the front of his pants.

The deputies tried to run, but she moved quick, propelled by myriad legs over the side of the platform, spinning and rolling effortlessly over the terrain. She was on top of them in a heartbeat, legs slashing and tearing, meat and blubber flying this way and that, spraying the four deputies over the trees and the forest floor. She slurped them up with her gashes of mouths, one on her head and one on the belly. Both sucked like vacuums, clearing the area of any evidence of man.

Mayor Bill suffered, but only briefly. She inched her way to him, savoring his shrieks and pleads for mercy. Once atop his body, her teeth and legs ripped away his clothing, leaving him exposed and vulnerable.

"Billy," she hissed from deep in her belly. "Billy boy, Billy boy..." she chanted, voices from the mouth on her head and the one on her belly chanting in slightly different tones, a dissonant duet. Her top mouth sealed over Mayor Bill's, sucking in and swallowing his breath, while the lower mouth enveloped his shaft, nibbling it a few times before excising it in one swift chomp. Bill screamed down into her belly, but the top mouth bit too, tearing away his lower jaw and half his throat.

Big Sammy's sobs were audible and raucous. She coiled off Bill's body and turned to face the noise.

Big Sammy thought she still had the most amazing eyes, one at the head and one in her new navel, emerald and full of fire.

The human myriapod in front of him inched closer, peeling herself off the ground until her body was half-erect, standing at his height and looking him in the eye.

"Not hungry anymore," she said, pressing close to his face, legs vibrating off his stubble, caressing his chest and arms.

"Not lonely anymore."

Her eye winked.

Her legs fluttered.

She coiled over backwards, curling onto the ground and skittering off into the trees, leaving a trail of slime and blood in her wake.

Big Sammy wavered on his feet. A sudden chill came over him, from fear, from shock, from the air rustling through the surrounding trees. The cold drew his attention to the warmth between his legs; he had soiled his britches. He didn't even care. He walked in circles for a moment, reliving the death, finding remnants of carnage he couldn't quite believe.

A touch.

A wiggle.

A tiny bite.

He slapped the back of his neck. Swiped at his arms. Ruffled his hands violently through his thick hair.

He could feel her, those legs, hundreds of feeling, violating, quivering legs over his body...

Big Sammy tore away his clothing, screaming and hollering as he gave it to the forest, then examined his body, intent on squashing each and every insect crawling on his flesh.

Clear. Rough, callused, hairy, but clear. No legs, no mouths, no bugs.

But beneath...

Big Sammy's upper thighs and groin were moving, hundreds of something squirming and wiggling beneath his flesh. He fell to the ground, clawing at his skin, desperate to release the poison she had given him in her cell. He lunged over to Bill's body, grabbing the Bowie knife from beside, and cut his inner thigh to examine the intruders beneath his skin.

"What the—"

No.

Not intruders.

Legs, all attached to his core, waiting to be freed.

His eyes caught the glimmer of the woman's trail of blood and slime, the moonlight illuminating his new path.

The cabin didn't smell like death.

Should it? Abbie wondered.

Abbie scanned the room—a respite from the social down-fall of the world beyond the woods. A cabin, secluded in the embrace of the mountain, on a road rarely traveled when grasped in the claws of winter.

"Disgusting. Bloody sin," her partner said, his sagging uniform making him look like a toddler in daddy's clothes.

We find different things disgusting, I guess.

"You stumbled across this?" Abbie asked him, cocking a brow, her eyes glued to the bare feet warming in front of the hearth. Young feet, unmarred by mileage, glittered polish accentuating delicate toes.

"Noticed her purchasing medical supplies in town.

Followed her out here a couple times, saw the ladies coming and going."

"Lucky."

"Yep. Call it gentleman's intuition."

Or a witch hunt. Again.

Abbie's eyes left the feet alone on the bearskin rug and turned to the wrinkled face perched atop the stocky body propped on the couch.

"Ma'am?" Abbie said.

"Gracie, please," the woman said, hands wringing her own skin like a wet towel.

"*Doctor* Gracie?" Abbie asked.

"Indeed," the doctor said, offense flavouring her words. "I am no monster. Only a monster would do this without a medical license—"

"It's illegal," her partner snapped. "You're a fucking criminal. You aren't above the law."

Abbie raised a hand to cease his impending soap-box harangue.

"And you," Abbie said, nodding to the girl on the sofa. "What's your name?"

"Clara," the girl whispered through a veil of protective hair.

"Are you all right, Clara?"

"Yes ma'am," Clara said under her breath. She looked healthy—uncomfortable, but calm and pink. "I am now."

"Now?" Abbie asked.

"Yes," Clara said, looking at Doctor Gracie. The doctor nodded. "She saved me, Doctor Gracie did. I was in no position to have a child, and with the new laws—"

"In place for a reason," her partner spat. "You're a murderer," he said, and turned a venomous eye to Clara. "You're *both* murderers."

"Age old debate that needs no rehashing," Dr. Gracie said, dismissing the argument before it began. "That's why I operate the way I do."

"How's that?" Abbie asked, noting the doctor's hands, steady and sure, tools of life and death.

"It's sterile, it's safe, there's informed consent from the patient, if a reasonable age. They stay here at the cabin until they feel well enough to depart. A retreat, of sorts. That's the facade, anyhow."

A place of life restored, not taken, Abbie thought.

Abbie looked at her partner, the lips that spewed misogynistic rhetoric behind doors opened and closed alike, the cock of an entitled head full of tainted ideas that permeated society, stripping creatures more gash than shaft of control over their own flesh.

"You're a monster," he reiterated, "and a criminal. Your little operation is officially closed for business."

Abbie watched him, his hands reaching for the cold, steel cuffs on his belt, hands she had never welcomed but had felt, nonetheless. Groping, assaulting, controlling...

She heard him—his vile words, words that had cut her

gender so many times before, reducing them to no more than incubators and servants.

It felt good, the cold steel in her hand vibrating from the ejaculation of death-delivery. It was beautiful, the crimson release of death seeping from the hole in her partner's head.

Clara's hands shrouded her face, her gasp caught in air. The doctor was as she had been, sitting, head held high; only difference was she no longer wrung her hands.

"Here, let me help you clean this up," Abbie said, assessing the splatter of blood and brains.

"You already have," Dr. Gracie said, a squinting smile scrunching her already prominent wrinkles into welcoming crevices. "I'll clean up the bloody fool. I have the means and knowledge..." Her eyes shifted to Clara.

It felt better than good, the freedom Abbie granted Doctor Gracie. Clara. *The girls, the women... herself.* Though small in scope, it was something. A shallow breath back into the lungs of civil, respectful humanity. Abbie stepped forward and kissed the old woman on the cheek.

"Carry on," Abbie said, holstering her weapon and walking out the door.

usalia pounded her fists into the ground, granules breaching the delicate epidermis floating loosely above the rubbery bones of her knuckles. She bled, cold and black, but didn't care. She was mad, no, *infuriated*, a rage hotter than she could ever have imagined possible. Futile were her efforts to communicate, to reason with the insanity mounting around her every day, the brash ignorance of those in charge and those not. The world was collapsing, but no mind was paid to that catastrophic fact. They were more concerned with battling each other than banding together. So she pounded.

"Having a good day, then?" asked a voice that floated in behind her.

She stopped pounding.

"Like every day, Ethril," she said.

She liked Ethril. He was one of the good ones, the sensible ones. He listened, really listened, with his heart and his mind.

"Life is not so glum, Rusalia," he said, grooving a spot next to her. "You think too large."

"How can I not?" Rusalia said. "Large is what will crush us. Large is bearing down on us, threatening our existence. Extinction, Ethril. Do you understand that?"

He pondered that for a moment though the smile never left his lips. She looked at him with jealous disdain. How can he be so peaceful, so settled? she wondered. They weren't long for their world, and their world not long for them. She knew that, deep down to her core. They were careening towards an end, an end brought about by forces unknown, a menace that would swallow them whole.

"We needn't worry about being snuffed out just yet," Ethril said. "Or at all, really. Why not just let it be, quit scrambling and enjoy the lifetime upon us?"

"Don't you worry?"

"Not even a little."

"What about future generations?"

"What of them? Do you know them?"

"No, but—"

"Will you create them, lay with me now?"

Her pallid cheeks flushed a simmering burgundy. Despite insinuations and expectations, she was not merely a vessel of procreation. That was not her purpose. There was more to her than that.

"I won't," she said.

"Well, then. You as an individual are unlikely to bear witness to the last beat of the last heart, so relax. Enjoy what is, not what might be. Besides, no one really knows what's going on. Could be nothing"

She sighed. He was right. It was probably nothing. Probably. Then again, something was up there, disturbing their world, wreaking havoc and social upheaval and physical decay. No one had seen it—or them—they could only imagine what they were, these things that visited from the dark corners of the shadows, breathing foul breath that clouded their vision and clawed at their lungs.

"I know you're scared, Rusalia," he said, more solemn now. "We all are. It's the boogeyman of our generation, you see. Everyone has one, a monster of sorts. This one happens to be ours. It will linger, engorged by the power of a million imaginations, but no one will see it clearly, and we will never know if it was even there."

"But the dead," she reminded him.

He was quiet. She saw hesitation in his eyes.

"There is that," he said.

Hundreds presumed dead, disappeared into the sky, the only evidence of their demise the occasional falling dismembered limb. Parts, shredded and separated, littered the land at regular intervals when the mass appeared.

"This will pass before you know it," he said. "The Policija will look into it, and they will take care of it."

"Cover it up, you mean."

"Maybe so. They need to do what they can to quash panic."

He's right, she thought. Would society be able to handle the truth of the monster if it was in fact as grand and menacing as the scientists surmised? Politicians felt it better to coat the truth in sugar before sweeping it under the rug.

"I think it tells us something exciting, though. That there is more to life than this," he said, sweeping a long, glistening limb in a partial pirouette. "More than us."

He looked upwards, and she followed suit. The world, the universe. So substantial and inconceivable to even the most learned of minds. Completely unfathomable to theirs. This invader, the monstrosity that lurked above their territory. Where had it come from? What did it want? An alien, thus far faceless and nameless, with intentions and demeanor unknown.

"I have to go," he said. "Settle yourself and go about your business. Never mind this foolishness. It has happened before, and it will happen again."

"Sure, yeah," she said.

He leaned in and brushed his lips over hers, nothing more than a delicate friction of their tender skin. Should have driven her wild, but it didn't. Her mind lay much higher than the white lips on his pale face. She moved towards home. Her parents would be worried, especially with the giant in the sky returning again. No one could decipher what the dark mass in the sky was, but it was there nonetheless. And with it came darkness, movement, death.

Rusalia went home. Like she always did.

Rusalia's eyes burned as she scurried through the darkness, weaving in and out of tunnels, skirting the gaze of trespassing eyes lurking on every surface. It was as if they knew. In her haste she failed to detect the obtrusive arm of flora jutting from the vine at her feet and it caught hold, latching onto her. Her body came crashing down, face submerging in the sand. She lay there for several minutes, actually hoping the ground would swallow her whole, digest her and absorb her into another world, a world that made sense.

"Rusalia?"

Ethril again. His voice sweetened her night and calmed her splintering nerves. It also elevated her anxiety, for she knew he was the only thing that could change her mind.

"Rusalia, are you all right?" he said.

"Not so loud," she whispered.

He looked at her with a scowl that pierced her heart.

"I know you don't approve," she said, struggling to move upright. "This is something so much bigger than us, Ethril."

He helped her up and pulled her close to his body. She

felt his pulse hammer against her chest, and his skin on hers, smooth and cool, enticing and sensual.

"Just stay here with me," he pleaded. "Forget this bullshit. What's your end game, anyways? Let's say you do find something. What will you do? Stay up there and play house with the aliens, then?"

The aliens.

They had moved closer, suspended in the sky, watching.

"Do you hate it here that much?" Ethril said, seemingly reading her mind.

"Hate is a strong word," she said.

So is dissatisfied, complacent, she thought. *Ignorant.*

"You may be content to muddle along, blissfully unaware," she said, "but I am no longer satisfied. I am afraid, and I am curious."

"Curious?" he said. "Curious enough to risk your life for something you don't understand? Hell, leave it to the professionals, won't you? There are teams looking into this, how to get up there safely."

"Red tape and political posturing. It appeases the masses, posturing like something's actually being done, when no one's actually doing anything."

Ethril rubbed his brow, his face loosening in woeful resignation. "It's dangerous, you know."

"It's dangerous here," Rusalia said. "Turning a blind eye is dangerous."

"It's cowardice, what takes you skyward," Ethril snapped.

"Stay here, brave this invasion, let things settle back to the way they used to be."

"I must go," she said. "If cowardice is what takes me there, fine. If bravery keeps me here, stagnant, living in fear, then I am more suited to be a coward. And a shining one I will be."

Ethril turned his face, and Rusalia swore she saw the glimmer of a tear lift from his eye.

Rusalia controlled her pulse, conducting its rapid staccato to a smooth legato with carefully conscious breaths. Panic would not serve well as a co-captain on the already arduous journey.

"Are you not the least bit curious?" she asked.

"Are you not the least bit afraid?" he asked.

"Yes," she said. "It's why I leave."

He resigned, embracing her for several moments past comfort, reluctant to release her to the unknown. She pulled away, looking into his white, glassy eyes, searching for an anchor to keep her home, in his arms, in the familiar.

"I love you, Rusalia."

He stayed suspended in place, fingers laced around the back of her smooth head, and leaned forward to seal his mouth around hers. They stayed locked together for minutes, neither wanting to release.

Finally, she pushed off. "And I, you, Ethril," she said as she moved away.

She harnessed her ride, taking care to focus on the reedy reins rather than Ethril's wounded eyes. As she mounted and rode away, she didn't turn. She couldn't. Her eyes and mind stayed trained forward and up on the black mass that loomed above, threatening to crush her heart and spirit. Or free it.

RUSALIA RODE hard for countless kilometers, her mount's shimmering flesh chaffing the insides of her bare thighs from the haste at which she pressed on. After a half-day's journey she was below it, gazing up at the mass that eclipsed the sun.

"This is it, boy," she said to her steed, patting his side. He responded, wriggling beneath her and moving in a circle. She tensed the reins, cocking his head to the sky. He resisted, his natural inclination remaining horizontal. It was all he had known when mounted by a rider.

"Up, boy. Up we go."

And up they went. It took them the better part of an hour to smooth out the kinks of vertical momentum, but once they had it down, they moved at a fair clip, the mass growing larger as they approached.

"It will be fine, boy," she said to the beast trembling between her legs. "We will get to them, meet them, and it will be magical. Then I will return to Ethril, love him and bear his children, and we will live in a world fresh with knowledge and possibility."

Her face darkened as her ride cantered forwards, thoughts of her own world clouding her dreams of the new. "Or perhaps we will bring back with us great tales of our travels, then return to the world above and bring Ethril with us, live with a society much more socially and physically advanced than our own. Yes, that's it."

And on they plowed, though the air grew warmer and thicker, a heavy pressure bearing down on her flesh, compressing her bones. As the kilometers passed, the pressure intensified, the light from the nearing sun began to sear her eyes, and the change in temperature was more than she could bear. She opted to wait out the daylight and travel in the solace of the moon. She maneuvered her steed to a nearby rock formation, guiding him into a cranny that would provide them shelter until nightfall.

"Let us rest," she said. "We shall not sleep tonight, so we rest now."

Bright turned to dim, then dimmer still, and Rusalia's anticipation swelled. She wanted to be on the move again but the sun's illumination still peeked around the black mass like silver eyelashes. But with the night came natural predators, eyes that cut through the dark, feeling the movement, ready to lunge.

But the predator above loomed heavier than the ones around, and the burning exposure of the sun the biggest threat of them all.

I must rest now, act later, she thought as she zoned into a trance, her pulse slowing and movements quieting to near still. As she settled into her resting dream, the world around shifted, distorted and displaced. She wriggled into consciousness, moving to the mouth of the cranny just in time to see it.

Rows of tightly woven braids floated down, gently falling geometric shapes unravelling from the belly of the beast above. It was like nothing she had ever seen.

Beautiful, she thought, jaw slack with wonder as the ethereal strands dropped out of sight, glimmering with the last kiss of the sun.

What are they? she thought, wonder that was slowly usurped by fear.

The jolt was sudden. The braids fluttering past her like binds of feathers fluttering to the land seemed to take hours on the journey down, but returned with gusto, slicing though the air, knocking her back with the force of their sudden and rapid ascent. She gasped as the black mass above sucked up the beautiful strands, drawing up to its mouth like a gluttonous predator.

A storm of displacement swirled around her, dust and

debris, plants and animals disturbed by the intrusion. After a time, the chaos settled, and all was still.

Until they started falling.

She didn't know how many had fallen before she noticed.

Stark white limbs, bloodied and ravaged and torn, falling to the ground like crimson-stained shards of snow.

And a head. Caught in an eternal scream, severed at the throat, tendrils of flesh floating behind like kite strings.

Then many heads.

Screaming.

Falling from above.

Rusalia released her terror in a silent howl that resonated towards her fallen tribe.

"We must go. Now."

Rusalia harnessed her steed once more, hauling him out of restful stasis. He chuffed and resisted, but relented after sensing her urgency. Her panic.

And up they went again. The burning silver lashes had rotated, giving way for the silver bath of the moon. Though still warmer than she would have preferred, early night would not boil the blood from her body. She had to get there. She had to know what the horrible dark mass was, what it was doing, what it wanted. Anger had replaced curiosity, bringing with it a chaser of vengeance.

It must be stopped.

WHEN THEY REACHED IT, it was still and lifeless, silent and dead, suspended in the air. Sounds came from above, from within; she heard a chittering of beings, muffled and manic, pitches and cadence unfamiliar to her ears. Rusalia was afraid but determined. And brave. She reached out a finger, long and pointed, skin clear and soft and delicate. She ran that finger along the beast, tickling its belly and feeling its flesh.

It was cold and hard, unresponsive. *It is their ship,* she thought, unsurprised. *They are within.*

But she could not see an opening. She drove her heel into her steed's rib, urging him upwards, but he would not budge.

"Now, boy, let's go! We must!"

We can't, he replied, apologizing with heavy eyes.

She was about to scold him, to release her anger and frustration by schooling him, but she didn't get the chance.

They came again.

The braids swooped past her, one caressing her cheek on the way down. She reached out, cupping her hand around it as it passed, its slick surface gliding through her loose grasp.

So peaceful. So lovely.

But she knew what was coming. She pushed off of her steed, moving to the side, and she waited. Waited for the break, the disruption, the mad upward sweep. When it came, she was ready, arms extended, claws waiting to connect. She latched onto a passing braid as it swooped up to the sky, hauling her with a velocity that snapped her spine and bent her head back to her should blades. But she held fast, wrapping her wispy thighs around the coarse braiding.

The final moments of her life were a blur. She didn't understand it, not once, even at her end. The braids catapulted her above a surface she didn't know was there, to a land she didn't know was possible. The atmosphere above that surface was unforgiving and harsh, sucking the oxygen from her lungs and pursing her skin. She couldn't breathe in this new air. The braids had breached the hull of the dark mass just as her hands flew to her sides. She gasped, madly trying to suck in air that never came. She dropped onto a surface that was hard and sharp and ripe with stench. Her jellied skin tore from her body as she flailed and flopped, trying to grasp onto the life that remained. She saw them, the aliens, tall and hairy, five tiny limbs stunted and hanging from longer limbs attached to vertical bodies. They were bellowing and nattering in a language she didn't understand, speech she heard through her ears, not her mind.

As her heart slowed and her chest clenched, she allowed her vision to rest along the surface of the vessel, grainy and splintered and brown.

That's when she saw him.

Ethril, splayed out on the deck, clasping his chest very much like she was.

An alien bent its lower limb, resting a bulbous joint upon the ground as it hoisted Ethril into the air. Ethril did not squirm as the alien took its blade, a short sword soiled in scales and fat and flesh, and sliced off Ethril's limbs and head in a mere flew flicks of its jointed limb. It pinched Ethril's head between its massive digits, looking him right in his dead eyes.

"C'mon, Ernest," a voice boomed. "Get 'er done! Pitch it to the drink and move on!"

And with a flick of that mangled, rough, ugly digit, Ethril's head careened over the side of the vessel, hitting the surface below with an audible plip.

Rusalia wept, her salty tears reminding her of home, of life, of a world she wished she hadn't taken for granted.

She wept and wished for the deep, the cold, for ignorance.

And her mind came to rest on what was below.

THE BANDAGE MAN

The backpack was the worst.

Sure, there was a lot of other stuff going on. Broken bones, a concussion, ruptured spleen among other things. But I felt none of that. As I slid down the pavement at what felt like a million kilometers an hour, I honed in on the edge of my laptop digging into my shoulder blade.

Turns out it was more angel than irritation. Had I not been wearing my backpack with my heavy-duty laptop inside, I would have snapped in two. Instead, it jammed against my scapula, preventing me from rolling and flopping down the freeway and cracking my neck.

Though, if I hadn't been wearing my laptop, I wouldn't have been going to work. If I hadn't been going to work, I wouldn't have been behind that fucking truck with his unsecured load, and that bale of fucking hay wouldn't have struck me in the chest, knocking me clear off my bike at 100 kilometers an hour.

So there's that.

What I would later come to realize was that the backpack was the least of my problems. The shattered collarbone, the splintered ribs, the gashed thighs and bruises and lacerations —barely problems at all. What was a problem was that spark. The spark that claimed my normal. They weren't sure if it was from my bike, the fuel, another vehicle, the battery from the laptop. Perhaps it was ash from a passing cigarette. Whatever the origin, that spark decided my life would take a very different path.

"How are we holding up today?"

I didn't answer her. I never answered any of the nurses. Or the doctors. I couldn't.

Meredith.

The nurses eyes dropped to her shoes. Like they always did.

"I'm sure she'll be along, once she's got a chance."

A chance.

The nurse fiddled with the IV tubing, took my vitals, avoided eye contact. She scratched something onto my chart, and the second nurse came into the room.

"Ready, Mr. Tremblay?"

Mr. Tremblay. Like I'm an invalid, an old man confined to a home.

Suppose I am.

I nodded.

It hurt.

I shimmied off the bed and onto the gurney. The wheels squeaked, taunting me as the staff wheeled me to the bathing chamber. Once a day, to replace old gauze with new, to slough off the old flesh and make way for the creature below.

The pain was excruciating, I think. Not sure. The cloak of morphine around my head helped a great deal.

ANOTHER DAY, another dollar.

For them, at least.

"You need to eat something, Mr. Tremblay."

They had taken the intravenous feeding tube out a week ago. They were aggressive about my nutritional intake. Turns out growing new skin is a helluva workout.

I sucked back the slop they provided, tasting nothing. The heaviness of the food sat high atop my gorge, but I willed it to stay down. I needed to get better, to grow into myself again.

She was coming.

THE GRASS WAS GREEN, and the willows wept tendrils of foliage in the midday sun. It was a gorgeous summer day, and

the view from my window splendid. Greens, blues, browns...
Eden.

But the most beautiful part was to come.

"Mr. Tremblay?"

I turned my head, barely noticing the taut stretch of my healing skin.

"She's here, Mr. Tremblay."

She spilled into the room, a swath of sunlight, dulling everything around her. Her brunette curls bounced against her face, and her hips swayed beneath her sheer paisley sundress. I closed my eyes for a moment, feeling those thighs against mine, those slender hands through my hair.

When I opened my eyes, I looked at her. Into her.

But she was elsewhere. Her icy blue eyes were everywhere but on mine, examining the bed, the curtains, the monitors.

The nurse patted Meredith's shoulder, gave her a long, hard look, then left the room without a word.

As the door closed, the room engulfed in a backdraft of silence. Meredith had stopped a few feet short of the bed, across the room from the window where I sat. I tried to stand, but my flesh complained, keeping me seated. I tried again, grasping the arms of the chair and pushing up on the wads of dressing over my hands, but my muscles had become unaccustomed to independent use.

"Don't get up," she said.

Don't get up. Two months, and that's what I get.

Don't get up.

She hesitated a moment, then sat on the side of the bed.

Closer, please.

She folded her hands in her lap, delicate fingers fiddling with the embroidery on her dress. Those fingers used to stroke my face, caressing my own fingers when I had been stressed about my transfer or the health of my ailing parents.

Touch my hands, now.

Please.

"You look well," she said.

I cocked my head.

I'm a mass of bandages. Is it the bandages that look well? Properly manufactured and functional?

I made a noise, tried to speak, but all that emerged were wet gargles from my crushed larynx.

Too bad I had been too cool to wear my helmet properly.

Too bad it tipped off and slid to the back of my head.

Too bad that fucking strap strangled me as I slid down the road on my back.

My head was saved, I guess. The reaper claimed my voice instead.

"Tom..."

Meredith's words failed her. Her lip quivered and she raised her eyes to mine. They were so blue against the backdrop of red, eyes that had shed months of tears.

I grunted. I pointed my finger at her, at her fingers, willing them to touch me, to feel me, to love me.

They moved, but only on themselves, stroking each other, settling her anxiety.

Her anxiety.

Not mine.

"Tom, this is so hard."

Don't I fucking know it.

"I... I'm so sorry."

What?

"You'll have the house, of course. Everything you need. I just can't..."

What?

"I can't. I'm sorry."

I sucked in a deep breath, trying to find the hair that had been knocked out of me.

She left without another word, leaving a waft of her scent in her wake, and the colours of her hair swirling in my tears.

The house was cold and empty. It was all there—the furniture, the art on the walls, the baby grand—but it was as empty as a black hole waiting to swallow me up and teleport me to the bowels of hell. It hadn't changed a bit—that is to say, I hadn't changed a thing since I had arrived home from the hospital a month before. Every picture, every book, every blanket. Exactly as we'd left it before I came off that bike.

She was gone, though. Her and her belongings. Just the

personals—her clothes, her mementos. She left most of the life we had created behind.

The doorbell rang, and my heart burst against my ribs. The sound resonated in my skull, whining around like a pinball. I took four long, loping strides to reach the door before the buzzer went off again. I couldn't handle the noise.

"G'day, Mr. Tremblay."

He didn't look at me. He held out the steaming, soggy pizza box, and examined the laces on his shoes.

I handed him the cash and waved him away. He could keep my extra few dollars for his minimal effort.

You couldn't even chat with me, could you? Not a single word, the weather, something.

He was already in his car before the thoughts finished in my head.

I slammed the door and tossed the pizza box down on the coffee table. I hoped that, wherever she was, Meredith was cringing about that hot, damp cardboard box sitting upon the naked wood, discoloring that cherry stain she liked so much.

I hope you feel it, you bitch.

I shivered. It wasn't all that cold outside, a decent autumn day, but it might as well have been the bleak midwinter right smack in the middle of that living room.

Me and my new skin, we were always cold.

I went to the kitchen and poured myself two, then three, no, four fingers of bourbon. There was a slight chance it would warm my blood, but either way, I wouldn't feel the cold anymore.

I set my glass on the coffee table, smirking at the moisture bleeding a ring into the wood, and cocooned myself in the blanket on the couch. I reached my hands out, one for the pizza and one for the drink, and retreated into my shell.

THE REFLECTION in the mirror was broken.

I stood there, looking at the clear patch where I had swiped my hand through the steam from the shower, and stared at the creation that was supposed to be me. Tattered, wrinkled, scarred. A shriveled concoction that would never quite be me.

No doubt she left you, you fucking Frankenstein.

The mirror did not survive the wrath of my fist.

My knuckles dripped globs of blood to the floor as I stormed through the house, smashing mirror after mirror, even the glass on the kitchen curio. I couldn't see me anymore. I was never meant to be. They shouldn't have played God. They should have let me be, let me fry to my end on that blacktop.

I collapsed on the couch, sobbing, the tears running down grafts healed over grafts on my cheeks, my knuckles pulsating with mild pain. I looked at the glass protruding from my flesh, shards pointed straight at my eye.

I turned away. I didn't want to see, not even in those tiny fragments of mirror.

I plucked them out as best I could by feel, wrapped my hand in a dish towel, and left.

THE LID over my glass eye twitched under the fluorescent lights of Barry's Drugmart, as if my artificial oculus was somehow offended by that flickering bulb. I stared at the shelves and displays of bandages, then looked at my hand wrapped in the dishtowel, crimson seeping wider every time I made a fist. I caught a movement in my eye, and turned to find a little girl, couldn't have been more than six years old, staring up the aisle at me, eyes wide with terror, mouth frozen in a silent scream.

I screamed, too.

I screamed, and swiped the shelf full of gauze and bandages and wrap and tape into my shopping basket until it was spilling over the sides. People gawked as I made my way to the counter, and sorted out the packages and boxes and sleeves one by one. They watched as I paid for my generous cache of first aid supplies.

They are wondering what I'll do with all of this. Am I healing? Am I preparing for further procedures? Have I lost my fucking mind?

I wondered too.

I WAS OILED AND SHINY, my unnatural flesh reflecting the flickering of the candles in my bathroom. The empty bottle of bourbon lay at my feet, a few of its final offerings soaking into the bandages that encased my toes. I had made it up to groin, and hesitated only a moment before wrapping my cock in gauze and taping it across my abdomen.

Twirling, spinning, contorting like a ballerina, I spooled myself in bandages, tape here there and everywhere to hold the dressings firmly in place. When all was covered but my single, working eye, I stopped. I stopped moving, and felt my body, packed tightly under layers of gauze and bandages, stiff and rigid and warm.

Not a monster now. I'm just healing. I'll heal.

I THOUGHT it odd there was no smell.

I woke up the next day, and many days after that, but the house smelled like it had the minute I arrived home from the hospital. The bandages were still on, some drooping, some yellowed with wear, some stained with the leavings of pizza and bourbon, but they had stayed in place, day after day, week after week.

But there was no smell.

I made no effort to shower, to relive myself in the toilet

where I should have, to brush what teeth I had left in my head or clean the spots that were sweaty and dank.

I just sat, festering in my bandages, healing.

People were less horrified by this. I went to the store, clothes over my bandages, and people looked at me with hope in their eyes. Hope that I was, in fact, healing. That repair was transpiring beneath the shroud of bandages.

Not like before. Not like when they saw me, skin patched together, fusing and growing and stretching. I was a burn victim, then. No hope of recovery. Pity, sadness, fear...

But now...

I walked through the grocery store, dressed in a fine pair of jeans and a button-down shirt, my bandages lying to everyone. I selected my beverages, fruits and veggies to aid my improving health, some crackers to help the bourbon go down easier.

That grocery store ruined my life all over again.

While I was there, crackers in hand, minding my own business behind my new creation of self, she floated in on a cloud, people smiling at her glow.

Meredith, hair flowing and lips curved in a bright smile, strolling the aisles as if nothing wretched had ever befallen her in her entire life.

I followed her, watching her slender fingers grasping boxes and packages, squeezing fruit, and patting bread to test for freshness.

Those hands should have been touching me.

I had to see those eyes, to see if the redness was there, blaring her ache for all to see, speaking of the tears she had shed for me every day and every night.

I touched her arm. She turned.

Her eyes were shocked, but they were not red. They were bright blue, and she really was glowing.

And those fingers. Those long, beautiful fingers with the smoky lavender polish. I couldn't quit staring at those fingers as they cupped around her belly. A belly that was round and plump and protruding between us like a weapon.

"Tom," she gasped as her hand circled the bump on her body. "I…"

I screamed. Behind my gauze, into my mummified shell, I screamed as I dropped my basket of groceries, dodging the apples rolling on the floor as I stumbled out the door and into the doom of the day.

I WAS TREMBLING. Not from cold—I was burning hot—but from rage, from jealousy, from loss. She was happy. Her life had not ended. She moved on, straight away, leaving me to rot and suffer on my own.

Who does it belong to, that baby inside her?

She didn't waste much time, now did she?

The realization hit me like a truck.

She wasn't coming back.

Things would never be the same.

No one would ever want me, ever again.

I was simply waiting to die.

I went into the bathroom, grabbed either side of the sink with my bandage-claws, and stared into the porcelain. The sink was still full of glass shards from the mirror above, most small, but a few just big enough. I grabbed the largest one and sat on the edge of the bathtub, clutching it in my hand like a dagger.

I didn't cry. I didn't feel like crying. I felt nothing. No anxiety, no loss, no sadness. I felt relief. An eerie calm. An acceptance.

I slashed.

Without hesitation, I closed my eye, lifted the mirror shard into the air, and kept hacking at my forearm, feeling the sharp edge driving deeper and deeper through the gauze and bandages. I became aroused beneath my dressings as I anticipated the pain from when the glass actually met my flesh, and the relief that pain would bring.

But it did not come.

I stabbed the mirror shard in, pulling and pressing through the dressings harder, faster. And when the mirror shard shattered into unusable pieces, I fetched a butcher knife from the block in the kitchen, and stabbed and sawed, drool and tears seeping through the bandages on my face as I turned feral, manic, desperate.

But I cut no flesh.

I went deep, straight through to the other side in some placess, but found no organic purchase. No flesh, no bone, no blood.

I slumped to the kitchen floor, staring at the gap in my arm. A wide laceration, clean and white, from the crook of my elbow to the heel of my hand. I poked the knife in and twisted, spreading the gap until I could see through my arm to the floor below.

Bandages.

All and only bandages.

I was layers of them, wrapped tightly, forming the shape of an arm.

The gleam of the knife in my hand caught my attention. I looked at my reflection. A sculpture of bandages with one eye peering out into the world.

I drove the knife into my throat, hilt deep. I felt nothing. I tugged and jiggled the blade, pulling and tearing and pushing, writhing on the floor to get the blade through until it reached my groin. Once the blade was liberated, exploding through the gash between my legs, I tossed it across the kitchen and drove my hands into my body. I pulled back the bandages, and found more of the same. Tightly packed layers of bandages, from my front to my back, from ribcage to spine. And nothing but. No bones, no organs, no blood.

I stopped. I breathed. I felt the breath expanding my belly and my heart beating against the pressure points in my body.

I felt good.

I felt new.

MY HOODIE COVERED my gaping body and open arm as I raided the first aide aisle of the local market. I cleaned them out of bandages, then moved to the next store, and bought all of theirs, too.

My house was fully stocked and then some when I returned to Barry's Drugmart.

Second Tuesday of the month.

She always refilled her prescription on the second Tuesday of the month, right before she went to work.

And she didn't disappoint.

I can't tell you how happy I was when she pulled into that parking lot.

How happy I was, the rag in my hand, the ether...

"MMMM."

It was almost seductive, that sound coming from her throat.

Her eyes flitted back and forth beneath her lids, struggling to break free, to see what and where and who was around her. I had bound her hands behind her back, but still she groped the air, feeling, searching for something familiar. I would have tied them in front of her so she didn't feel so exposed, so vulnerable, but that belly. That round, bulging life inside her...

She was cold. Gooseflesh rippled over her body and her nipples stood at attention, dark, swollen.

"Tom?"

I can't speak, my love.

"Tom, is that you?"

Can't speak, for the gauze is oh so dry.

"Tom, what's happening?"

I'll show you.

She sputtered, the liquid running down her hair, dripping into her eyes, her mouth, over her tongue.

That's when the screaming started. She knew. The smell, the taste... she knew what was dripping from her hair, what dampened her naked body.

It's okay, honey. It's quite amazing, really.

I set the needle down on the record, letting it spin and crackle until Mozart danced through the apartment and into our ears.

Meredith, my love, why do you struggle so? I'm only helping you to understand... to become... me.

The crescendo reached a peak as the flames caressed the petrol over her body, beginning her transformation.

"*O*h my word!"

Muriel clasped her chest, her face aching from the stretch of her sudden, surprised smile. The announcement choked from tinny speakers, reverberating off the booths and masses of people.

"Again, the winner is lucky number 48! C'mon down to the stage and claim your prize!"

Muriel lifted her tray again. The number 48 was there, all right, crudely scripted in red marker. Others around her in the food court were eating and mumbling to each other, indifferent to her luck.

Bloody fools, she thought, clucking her dry tongue. "These swine wouldn't know class and winning if it struck them square in their inbred noses."

She set her tray down and shifted the plate of chicken

fingers to the table, next to her boat of ranch. A few grunts and heaves later, she was out of her chair and comfortably seated on her Rascal, tray in hand.

"Stanley! Isn't this grand?"

Stanley continued eating his turkey leg, taking no notice of her glee.

"Ingrate," she snarled, adjusting her pearl necklace. "I'm tickled a fine shade of pink, thank you very much."

The Rascal whirred down the aisle toward the back of the arena where the announcer sat perched on the stage. Muriel passed booths with vendors pedaling long-lasting lip stain, homemade candles smelling of soft baked goods, and silver jewelry that caught the gleam of the spastic fluorescent lighting with glittering fervor. Muriel turned her nose up at the cheap baubles and trinkets, keeping one hand on her winning tray lest someone snatch her deserved prize.

Muriel beamed with callous pride, flashing the bottom of the winning tray at vendors as she passed. She teased her silver, perfectly permed hair with the tips of her manicured fingers.

No one smiled. No one acknowledged her win or her glee.

"Sour bunch, the lot of you," Muriel mumbled under her breath.

The air became warm and stagnant. Muriel swiped a hand across her forehead, beads of sweat smearing across her sagging skin.

"I'm positivity melting."

She looked at the vendors. They weren't smiling. They were scowling. Angry. Hateful. Some bared their teeth as she passed, others cussed at her in venomous whispers.

"Well I *never!*"

Muriel pushed on the throttle, willing the Rascal to go faster than it could. She was sweating profusely now, the armpits and thighs of her emerald velour track suit soaked with sweat. The smell of scented candles was far behind her, replaced by a bouquet of burnt hair and rotting meat. She gagged, her gorge bubbling acid and panic.

"What in the world—"

Now the vendors were smiling. Amused. Teeth sharp and elongated, blood dripping from cracked lips, mouths stretched and torn from ear to ear. Muriel's heart beat a forceful staccato against her rib cage, her pulse cymbals smashing inside her head.

The Rascal would go no faster. She abandoned it, grunts leaking out of her as she bore her own weight. The beasts mocked her, grunting and groaning, mimicking her strain.

"Sweet baby Jesus," she mewled as she hurried away, pushing towards the stage as fast as her jiggling legs would carry her.

The vendors screamed, cawing like rabid banshees. They were hideous beasts with exposed ribcages and contorted spines, talons, and long, black tongues inserted in orifices both high and low. A salesman at a booth selling pots and pans was elbow deep in his own abdomen, ripping out his intestines and coiling them on the table. He saw her and giggled, bubbles of blood-tinged spittle dribbling off his cankered lips.

Muriel knew she was screaming. She could feel her stomach muscles straining and hot air moving across her tongue. Her voice, however, was drowned out by braying and profanity, violence and exuberant bloody coitus escalating all around her. Even the other attendees were tainted, rolling around on the floor at her feet, bones shattered and exposed, grabbing ahold of each other and eating the flesh off each others bones.

A young couple, no eyes in their sockets and flesh marred by deep talon gouges, were fornicating on the ground across the aisle. Muriel was too focused on the surrounding horror to notice the gore beneath. She tripped on the girl's legs and came crashing to the floor in a puddle of blood and human meat. She flailed, smearing blood angels on the concrete floor as ghouls and demons ripped and shredded her clothing until she was exposed and vulnerable.

She looked up for help, for understanding, for anything.

She found him, perched upon the stage, on a rotting throne made of bones and teeth bound together with strips of flesh and braids of hair.

"Welcome, lucky number 48! You are quite the lucky lady today!"

He was large, at least three meters tall, with rippling muscles on every inch of his gleaming crimson body. The horns on his head were coiled, tips gored into the sides of his head and exiting through his eyes. His tongue licked out like a serpent, black and thick and meaty, toying with the obsidian shaft between his legs.

"Congratulations on your win, Muriel," he said, in a chorus of tones, guttural words from the pit of his stomach.

Muriel wanted to run, to scream for help, to leave that trade show, never to return again. She was better than this. Than all of this.

She looked behind, way behind, to the place she had started her journey. Through a sea of writhing and gyrating monsters and a bath of blood and pain, she saw Stanley, screaming and sobbing.

And herself, splayed out on the floor, eyes wide and still. The trade show paramedics were pumping away on her chest and blasting breath into her mouth, but it was too late.

Muriel looked at the tray in her hands. That lucky number 48 stared back at her, a wolf in sheep's clothing.

Laughing.

WANT

The frisbee flew through the air, twinkling and twirling as it spun. Anne thought it looked very much like a UFO soaring in front of the clouds, its shape and rainbow of glittering colours imperceptible against the backdrop of the midday sun. She squinted and watched it fly by. It landed in the sand about four meters from where she was standing.

"Doofus!" Kyle ran by her, swatting her on the back of the head as he passed. "It's ain't sightseeing, Anne. You gotta jump for it! Now I'm really kickin' your ass!"

"Off you fuck," she said, flipping him the bird and returning to her towel laid out in the sand.

Akkoro's Cove was a utopia—glittering white sand beaches, turquoise waters, and exotic flora and fauna. It was an island off the northern coast of New Zealand, difficult to get to but amazing once there. Other than the resort—which housed about three hundred guests and half that in staff who lived on site—the island was secluded. The crowds, though still abundant, were thinner than they would have been in the middle of high season; it was a much smaller crowd than if it were at full capacity. Anne was thankful Kyle and Steph had chosen fall for their wedding instead of the dead of summer.

"You done for the day, lazy ass?" Kyle said, kicking sand at her as she reapplied a thick slathering of sunscreen.

"Done for now," she said. "My florescent white flesh can only handle so many rays at a time. Anyways, don't you have a wedding to prep for?"

Kyle plunked down in the sand next to Anne and gazed out at the water. "Nothing to do. Easy peasy, this beach matrimony business. Show up, drink rum, tie knot, more rum."

Anne smiled. "Steph feel the same way?"

"Sure does! She put all her energy into picking a dress back home. She's letting the resort take care of the rest. We just specified tropical flowers and marble cake, and the rest doesn't matter."

"Lovely," Anne said, looking out at the water.

And it was lovely. She was happy for her brother, happy on that beach, serene and peaceful in their little hidden corner of the world.

THE BASS from the discotheque thumped into the night air. Anne could feel it through the sand, vibrating up the soles of her bare feet. They danced and drank, drank and danced until all she could taste was rum and pineapple, and all she could see were the swirling, whirling lights strung through the groves of palm trees surrounding the resort. On her umpteenth trip to the loo, Anne sat on the toilet seat, head swaying and vision wavering. Her stomach started to do some pretty nifty gymnastics.

"Air," she muttered to herself, stumbling out of the stall and back onto the beach. The lights, pounding music, and chattering crowd merged together in a nauseating slurry, so she stumbled away from everything to an empty section of beach to regain some sobriety.

The air was warm but the wind from the ocean kept the temperature tolerable. The waves rolled softly against the shore, a rhythmic whisper that filled the night. Anne eased herself down into the sand, letting the water kiss her carefully manicured feet as she closed her eyes and drank in the full sensory experience of nature. She swayed with the breeze, her body lightly heaving with the surge of the waves, her mouth watering at the scent of coconuts and salt water. It was glorious.

Suddenly, the hair on Anne's arms stood at attention, sending a chill through her body. Her head rolled forward, and she opened her eyes, not expecting the darkness that greeted her. She looked back over her shoulder at the discotheque. The lights were tiny and far away, the music barely detectable beneath the sounds of nature.

Did I really walk that far? Seemed only a moment...

A low rumble caught her focus. She turned her head and came face to face with a pair of glowing purple eyes. As she opened her mouth to scream, something wrapped around her leg and dragged her into the water. Her scream filled with a full gulp of the sea, and she struggled to find the ground, a buoy, anything she could grab ahold of to avoid being dragged to her death.

Lower and lower she went, until her ears popped and her chest ached, and in her mind, the frantic hum of panic threatened to drive her insane. She thought she might burst from the pressure, from the pain, from the fear, but an odd saving grace came out of nowhere.

A kiss, gentle and sweet, lingering and soft.

Then all fell still.

Anne opened her eyes and was once again greeting by that purple stare. The eyes were mesmerizing, sultry and haunting, long lashes waving in the water.

Then it occurred to her.

I can breathe.

She pushed back to get a good look at who or what had dragged her to the depths of darkness.

A woman, no, a *female*, silver flesh and indigo hair, floated and swayed in front of her. She had plump, black lips and a coy smile across her beautiful face. She was naked, her glittering silver breasts heaving with the water, and her labia was covered in thick, green moss.

But she had no limbs. Not in the traditional sense.

In place of legs and arms, she had tentacles, two for each appendage, eight in total. They coiled around her, writhing and caressing her body like lustful serpents, silver flesh and black suction cups kissing her face, her hair, her stomach. Anne startled when one reached out and caressed her cheek, the light suction of the cup tasting her ever so gently.

"Whooaaooo." Anne tried to speak, but couldn't form words under the water. She tapped her own chest and tried to yell. "Anne!"

Anne. The voice in her hand sounded musical, like a harp. *Pleased to meet you, Anne of the Land.*

Anne coughed and her heart clenched in her chest. She attempted to speak again. This time the words flowed easily through the water.

"Who are you?"

I am one who wants.

"Do you have a name?"

Only want.

"What do you want?"

The creature paused, her scaled, silver flesh bristling in the current. *Beauty.*

Anne laughed, and a bubble exploded from her mouth and rose towards the surface. "You want beauty? You?" Anne looked at the woman again, her flesh like glittering platinum, her mass of indigo hair that floated like thick smoke in the dark waters. Her curvaceous, luscious body. "You are gorgeous!"

Want beauty, the creature repeated. *Warmth, music, lights.*

Another tentacle came out and wrapped around Anne's waist, pulling the two of them together. Anne blushed as she felt the firmness of the creature's breasts, the heat off her groin, the slickness of her skin. The tentacles fluttered and quivered all around, wrapping themselves around Anne's arms and legs, caressing, rubbing, squeezing.

Want you.

Like the most euphoric release, Anne's body exploded in pleasure. She fell, tumbling and somersaulting, pulsating and screaming until the fresh night air slapped her in the face. She sucked in mighty gulps of air, trying to catch her breath, floundering to keep her head above the water. The shore was visible, the lights of the discotheque a beacon in the night. She swam, her muscles screaming at her the whole way, until she found sand and pulled herself onto the beach, exhausted, confused, and utterly spent.

"Tied one on pretty tight last night, eh?"

Kyle was grinning at her, obviously making every effort not to laugh out loud.

"Guess so," Anne said, tugging at the spaghetti strap of her bridesmaid's dress. "I could have used some more sleep, that's for sure."

"Perhaps you shouldn't have slept face down in the sand." Now he laughed, a hearty chortle punctuated by a slap on her back. She grimaced. "And yeah, yikes, that burn's not doing you any favours."

She looked at her shoulders in the mirror, a dark pink against the soft grey of the bridesmaid's dress. Thank fuck Steph had chosen simple and loose. There was only so much discomfort Anne could handle. It was going to be a long day. Her stomach roiled like the sea and her headache pounded behind her eyes.

She still could still feel the caress of those phantom tentacles on her flesh.

"Anne, what's wrong?"

Kyle took her hands and turned her away from the mirror. He wasn't smirking now. His eyes were scrunched in worry.

She drew a deep breath and exhaled slowly. "I'm perfectly fine. Just hungover, and shaken by bad dreams on the beach. Tentacled mermaid sex, and all that."

"Huh," Kyle said, contemplating. The smile was back.

"Forget that rubbish," Anne said, punching him on the shoulder. "Let's go get you married off."

"AND DO YOU, Kyle, take this lovely woman—"

Anne was amazed she hadn't toppled over two minutes into the ceremony. The sun was blaring down on them, the humidity hung thick in the air, and the smell of the flowers choked her with every breath. Kyle and Steph had written cute little vows that went on about ten minutes too long, followed by a sand ceremony where they mixed different colours together to signify unity.

Too long, Anne thought as she took calculated breaths and tugged at her dress.

She ached, both her muscles her mind. Everything. She wanted to crawl right out of her skin, slither her way back to her room, and hide under her blankets for the rest of the trip. She itched at her hair, which was caked in what felt like a liter of smoothing balm, and itched at her flaking, raw skin. Even the sand trapped in her sandals was torture; she swore she could feel each and every grain grinding into the soles of her feet, actually penetrating her flesh as her weight sunk her lower and lower into the ground...

"And I now pronounce you Husband and Wife. You may plant a big ol' smoochy on that bride of yours!"

The crowd laughed and cheered as Kyle and Steph embraced, signaling the end of a long and arduous ordeal.

WATER SPLASHED up on Anne's face as she vomited into the

toilet for the third time, her ribs and guts aching from the trauma. She was pleased, though, that she had made it through the brief receiving line before sprinting to the washrooms on the far side of the resort to lose her lunch. She didn't want to put a damper on the day by causing any scene or worry.

After what she was fairly certain was the final heave of her meager stomach contents, Anne got off her knees and exited the cramped stall. She washed her hands and splashed some water on her face, then looked in the mirror.

Death looked back.

Her skin was a sickly shade of grey, the whites of her eyes almost completely red from the violent vomiting. Her hair had been mussed out of its sleek side-bun and clung in straggly clumps to the side of her sweaty face. Her dress was scattered with wet spots—some from the vomit, the rest from the splash at the sink. She was a hot mess.

Twenty minutes of preening and fussing got her back to a half-presentable state, but she still looked and felt like ocean sewage. She itched at her shoulders, the irritation of the burn flaring up with the slightest touch. Against all common sense, she scratched, then scratched harder when her nails didn't satisfy. Before long she was frantic, clawing at her shoulders and back with vigor until her fingers were slick and wet.

No.

She brought her hands up to her face. They were covered

in blood, tendrils of flesh hanging from beneath her glittering nails.

"Oh shit, oh fucking fuck..."

She yanked some paper towel from the holder and began mopping up the mess. It was futile. The dress was stained in dark crimson, and skin was still peeling off her arms, chest, and shoulders. Thankfully, the sun was setting. It would be cooler now, so she could easily get away with donning a shrug.

"Get your shit together," Anne scolded herself.

She left the bathroom without another glance in the mirror.

THE EVENING DRAGGED ON, the revelry becoming a steady crescendo as the hours passed and the alcohol was consumed. Anne's head went from aching to throbbing to pounding, and every centimeter of her skin hurt. She was sore, tired, nauseated, and boiling hot. Didn't help matters that the evening was hot and humid, and the smells and sounds of the reception were overwhelming. Lights twinkled and flickered, glasses clinked, people laughed, and the pungent odor of hor dourves wafted through the air—a medley of deviled eggs, seafood, and buffalo wings.

Anne wasn't sure she could take much more of the assault on her senses.

"There you are, ol' girl!" Kyle said, slapping her on the back. She winced and pulled her shrug tight around her shoulders. "Geez, sis, sorry. You okay? You don't look so hot."

"I'm good," she said, forcing a smile. "But more importantly, how are you doing? Big day."

He didn't answer before she wrapped her arms around him and squeezed him tight. She felt an overwhelming love for her brother. Pride. Admiration.

Fear?

"Anne," he said, pulling back and taking her face in his hands. "Something's not right. And fuck this day, it's magical no matter what. Are you just hungover, or is there something else going on?"

"Hungover, I guess," she said, scratching at her stomach. "And I got too much sun, passed out in that sand. Maybe bug bites, I dunno."

"Have some food," he said, motioning at a tray of calamari on a nearby table. "Or better yet, hon, why don't you pack it in, call it a night."

"Kyle, I can't do that," she said, eyes welling with tears. "It's your wedding, for fuck's sake!"

"Anne. It's over now. We're all half-cut, you're suffering... go to bed. Join us tomorrow."

Anne clenched her fists as her stomach rolled again. A fresh wave of heat flooded her aching body. Unable to form the words for fear she might puke right on Kyle's face, she nodded. He kissed her on the cheek and turned back towards the crowd.

"Love ya, lightweight!" he called out as he walked away.

Love you too.

Anne turned from the crowd and started down the beach, heading to her room. Every step was a struggle, her muscles screaming and sweat pouring from her, dripping off her brow and trickling down the tip of her nose. She walked faster, but her chest began to hurt. She turned to go back, to get help, but her stomach seized, dropping her to her knees in a violent urge. She vomited into the sand, thick and heavy, and choked to catch her breath. Her vomit was clear, salty...

Ocean water.

She coughed, aspirated vomit rattling around in her lungs, and vomited again. This time, the vomit-water was tinged with blood. And lots of it. She tried to scream, but with noise came more water, and with water came blood.

And the heat. Her flesh was on fire, itching, burning. She was choking, trying to suck in air as if through a pinched straw. Her arms and legs were weak, too weak to carry her much further. Her room was too far in one direction and the party too far in the other. She was sick, hot, in pain...

She crawled on her hands and knees through the sand until she reached the water. Plunging in face-first, she drove her whole body in until she was submerged in the cooling blanket of the sea. The heat went out like a doused flame, and she felt release as her skin softened and calmed.

Then it came. Again. The familiar grasp coiled around her ankle, pulling her down, down, down.

When they finally stopped, a tentacle came up, its sharp tip lashing out and slicing Anne's throat. Black blood danced in the water in front of her face. Anne's fingers found her throat, and the gaping gash that allowed her to breathe.

Anne was in a daze—calm, confused, serene. The creature was there, tentacles feeling Anne's body, rubbing her flesh. The creature rubbed and rubbed, sloughing off strips of flesh that floated in front of Anne's face to the surface above. It caressed and pushed and pulled until Anne's skin had been stripped, leaving her with a glittering silver sheath where her flesh had once been.

"What's happening. Who am I..."

Anne stretched her arms and legs, her muscles releasing and bones creaking and cracking as they separated, making way for the tentacles that pushed from her core and out of her body, disposing of her former limbs with little more than a pop. Anne didn't even notice.

I want to go back. I want the lights, the music, Kyle...

The creature backed away, reaching out and snatching Anne's detached limbs with its tentacles, coiling around them and melding them to its body.

What is happening? Anne thought, a fog over her mind. *Those are mine. I want...*

Once the arms and legs were attached, the tentacles shriveled, turning to dust and dispersing into the abyss. Those purple eyes turned to blue and those black lips to a gentle shade of coral. Her smile grew, large and wicked, and she laughed. She laughed, and the ocean shook, the booming voice from her belly sending shockwaves to the ocean floor, quickening her rise to the surface. Anne watched her leave, those delicate pink feet kicking in the water, heading towards the surface. To the beach.

Anne swam upwards, staying just below the surface of the water because the lights and noise and smells hurt every fiber of her being. She watched as the woman with the indigo hair walked onto the beach, her silver dress draped over her pale skin. Anne watched as she walked towards the twinkling lights, the music, the happiness.

Want, Anne thought.

DEATH IS THE ANSWER

Death is the answer.

The dirt between Siobhan's teeth crunched like crystals of sugar, but they were earthy, not sweet.

She did not cry.

"What's the matter, baby?" the monster in the halter top and expensive Converse spat at her.

Siobhan didn't shout back.

"C'mon," the monster said, tendrils of blonde whipping out behind her as she turned and strode away, the herd following her like a stench.

"Death is the answer," Siobhan breathed through gritted teeth.

She stood, brushed the dirt off her new rainbow romper, and walked away from the schoolyard.

It hadn't been the first time she tasted dirt. It had nothing to do with the romper.

Behind her, she could hear the jeer and taunts of her peers, their not-so-subtle judgement, the humor at her expense. She clenched her fists until her nails were embedded in her palms, the trickle of blood dribbling down her lily-white hands mocking her as well.

Death is the answer.

She passed through her front door, evading her folks and sliding up the stairs to the solitude of her room. With door closed and curtains drawn, she released the dam, liberating the tears to flow freely down her bruised and battered cheeks.

But only for a moment.

Death is the answer.

Once the superficial sadness had been drained from her system, she opened the drapes and sat at her desk. The wood of her watercolor pencils felt euphoric against her calloused hands. She looked up at the mirror on her wall, at the discoloration forming beneath her bloodshot eyes, the rip in her romper, the nail marks on her arms.

Death is the answer.

And she drew.

She drew herself, that mousy brown hair, limp strands of moldy fibers falling over her shoulders. Her mosquito-bite breasts and pudgy tummy draped in an outdated outfit from Wal-Mart. She sketched herself crouched on the ground, shoulders slumped in defeat, her body weak and broken, tears streaming down an ugly face.

Siobhan stopped. She set the pencils down on her desk and stared at herself on the page.

Death is the answer.

"DIE!"

Tears exploded from her eyes, drenching the paper. With crimson pencil in hand, she slashed at the wet art, tearing herself to shreds, flaps of paper flesh flying this way at that, falling to the floor in a slurry of murder.

Her crying slowed. She forced herself to take a breath.

She slid another piece of paper in front of her.

Again, she drew. This time she used a wide swath of colors, vigorously sketching and shading and scratching until her middle finger was blistered and raw and her thumb ached. She created until the pencils all needed sharpening and the paper was beyond full and so was her heart.

Siobhan sat back. She stared at the picture, and an invisible string tugged the corners of her mouth into a smile. She took the shreds of crimson paper and laid it at the feet of her new art.

A girl looked back at her from the page. A woman. Large and tall and powerful, muscles gleaming through a rainbow romper. The woman stood tall on a mountainside, chest heaved and head held high, the whole world at her feet. In her hand, a weapon that could, would, and did conquer the world. A pencil, cocked and aimed at whoever dare cross her again.

The warrior stood atop her conquered foe, the pile of shredded flesh-paper; the weak and /'vulnerable Siobhan was no longer.

I am strong, the warrior said.

"I am strong," Siobhan repeated.

I am beautiful, the warrior said.

"I am beautiful," Siobhan repeated.

"I am me," Siobhan said.

"*Her* death was the answer."

NEED

My hands trembled. Not profusely enough to allude to an underlying physiological impairment—epilepsy, Parkinson's, or the like—but bad enough that I wasted precious drops of my overpriced caffeinated concoction over the report I had been pretending to write. Probably for the best. Caffeine was the nourishment my anxiety was craving.

"Need a bib?"

I almost jumped clear out of my skin. I looked towards the elevator, then back to the intruder, taking time to review the faces milling about the cubicles barricading me in the center of the suffocating bullpen.

"Geez, you on edge there, buddy?" he asked me.

I held onto my desk in a feeble attempt to ground myself, as if a piece of furniture could hold me down from the antigravity of my paranoia. *C'mon, Bruce. Calm the fuck down.*

"Sorry," I said, trying to appear sheepish and aloof. I imagine I came across as awkward and gassy. "A little burnt out, that's all."

"You look right frazzled," he said. "Too much on your plate? Can I offer you a hand, maybe take the Jones file from you?"

"No, no, nothing like that. Work's fine."

"Wife givin' you trouble? Kids acting up?"

Get away from me. "I'm fine, really. Just need a little sleep, is all."

"Okay," he said. "You sure, though, that I can't help with anything? You look wound tighter than virgin pussy."

"Look, it's nothing. Period."

He looked at me like a freshly slapped puppy. Poor Ed and I had been friends—at least of the professional persuasion—for all our years here with the company. Ed thought we were perfectly chummy, that he knew his old pal like the back of his hand. But he didn't. He didn't know what lurked inside me, writhing beneath the cover of my skin, creeping around within the folds of my brain. Ed took my curtness and swallowed it whole, and walked away in a sulky snit. *Sorry, buddy. Not up for banter today.*

Cue the sweats, which bled out my pores like hot sludge. I felt the need engulf me, wrap its boney fingers around my frail neck, and dig its fingernails into my pallid skin. *Be gone, evil thing, cravings of the beast! Why do you want me so?* The truth is there is no beast, no great unknown dangling me like a marionette on flimsy strings. It's all me. I'm the beast.

I had to get out. It was daylight—not the ideal time to sate my hunger—but I couldn't wait a moment longer. Granted, it would be riskier with the sun illuminating my activities, but the desire, the searing drive was threatening to rip me apart limb from limb. I closed my laptop, tidied my stack of papers into a neat pile to deposit them in the top box on my desk (the ever-nagging to do-box), and swiped my assortment of office paraphernalia into a desk drawer. I had to maintain an appearance of sanity, tidiness, and normality, lest people think I was deteriorating into some sort of head case. The less attention I drew to myself, the better. *Blend, Bruce. Just be normal.*

The elevator took two eternities to reach my floor. I felt the eyes of the office boring down on me, drilling holes through my skull and scapulas, peering deep into the recesses of my mind and heart. I turned, ready to confront the vessels of my judgment, and found all of the office lemmings sifting lackadaisically through their own piles of paper. They didn't have a clue. Good for them. Good for me.

Daylight. It should have felt warm. I should have been able to enjoy the rays on my pasty skin, but the plume of panic rising from my belly forbade me to enjoy anything whatsoever. I stumbled into the street like a cheap addict desperately seeking for his next fix. *Where to go, what to do?*

Let's find some wretched scum, some shit stack with lowered inhibitions and a bent moral compass. That's the dream, anyways. I hated to draw it out of some regular Johnny, a do-gooder with normal human impulses who could be driven to the unthinkable by unimaginable circumstances.

Bill's Pole, the local cue and brew. That's the place. What was once a hip-happenin' spot had deteriorated into a vile dive, catering to the likes of extreme right-wing hillbillies who chowed down on human rights for breakfast. Not hard to find a piece of shit in a toilet like that. The place was notorious for brawls, hate crimes, and sexual assault. Perfect.

I struggled to inhale as I walked through the barrier of smoke that greeted me just past the rusty doorway. Smoking had been banned in all establishments, but the police recognized a risk too big to enforce, thus steered clear of this futile target. The bar was half empty, but the half full aspect was promising; a smattering of rednecks well on their way to stumbling drunk, already ranting about new measures on gun control and health care initiatives. I took a deep breath, and engaged the most flamboyant stride my hips could waggle. I walked up to the greasiest oaf at the bar, the one with the calloused knuckles and nose busted sideways on his face. This guy was no stranger to a little confrontation. I sidled up next to him, and breathed heavily in his ear.

"I would love to feel you inside me, big boy," I cooed.

The stool flew out from under him, and he swung around,

acting like he had just taken a right hook to the jaw. He was speechless, and his friends were puzzled. Perfect.

"What? You don't remember me?" I said, drooping a sultry pout.

Now his friends weren't looking at me, they were looking at him. And he saw them looking.

"C'mon, I know we said we'd wait 'til tonight, but I'm ready now," I said, stroking the front of my pleated trousers.

His fists clenched, his lip trembled, his face turned red like it was a steaming kettle ready to scream. His friends sniggered and whispered to themselves, backing away from their kingpin as if the gay might be catching.

"Step down, queer," he growled under his breath. "I'm gonna give you the benefit of the doubt, seeing as you're obviously a bit simple in the head. You've clearly got me confused with someone else."

"No," I said confidently. "No, I don't. I remember your smell vividly. Your taste."

I stepped forward and licked him on the cheek.

The next few minutes were a blur. My brain rocked in my skull, my teeth tinkled to the floor like piano keys from a old cartoon, my knuckles bent back until my fingernails brushed the backs of my wrists. That coffee I had consumed at the office made an appearance, thrusting up from my stomach and coating the spit and grime riddled floor of Bill's Pole. Then I felt the sun again. I looked up through puffy eyelids and saw brick on either side of me, jutting up towards the sky. The back alley. This was very, very promising.

"Look," said a gruff voice.

I did look. I looked up and saw the face of my attacker, and no one else. We were alone in the alleyway, away from prying eyes and security cameras. Away from witnesses, with enough trash, drains, and privacy to eliminate evidence. Perfect.

"I don't know what your deal is, but you've fucked with the wrong guy. I know you're trying to get a rise outta me, and you got it. Now, if you know what's good for you, you'll skedaddle. If you pull this shit again, I'll mess you up. Again."

What?

"That's all you got, big boy?" I taunted.

This can't be it.

"It is, little man. You ain't had enough? Your face has been rearranged, and you'll be hurtin' for days, even weeks maybe. Count your blessings that's all you got."

My blessings would be worse.

"Are you some sort of chicken-shit?" I screeched at him.

He looked confused, flustered, but not angry. *Ah shit, this isn't gonna work. Unbelievable.*

"Run on, little queer. Go get your attention elsewhere."

The slamming of the metal door resonated off the brick walls framing the alley, and throbbed in my swelling head. I tried to catch my breath and stifle the impending tears. *Can't judge a book, they say.* I would have thought this one was enough of a wretch, or at least there was one buried deep inside, but some just don't have the capacity. I wish I could judge that better, and save myself the effort and hurt.

I peeled my broken body off the pavement, leaving patches of skin and bone scattered around like a voodoo alter. I brushed myself off, hopeless that relief would come on this day. I walked to try and distract my mind, to curb my aching, craving body, and then I saw it. I wasn't sure how long I had walked before it came into view. I saw it, and plan unfolded before my eyes.

THERE HE WAS. Blue sedan with football window decals, just as she had said. A man, a tall and thick man, just as she had described. He pulled up to the curb, and watched through his trendy transitions lenses, scanning the preteens flooding out of the intermediate school. I walked up to the car like it was my business, like I was doing something I should be, with a confidence in my step that surprised even me. I rapped on the tinted window.

"Mr. Winfred? Paul Winfred?"

He looked at me, then did a double take. I must have looked a frightful sight, my face busted up and my hands mangled into shattered claws. I had managed to snag a change of clothes from the thrift shop down the street, but not much could be done about the bodily damage.

"Can I help you?" he asked through a slightly lowered window.

"It's Tamara, sir," I said with the biggest kind of smile on my face. "She is an angel, sir."

He flew from the car, posturing like a rutting moose.

"What?" he said, panic caught in his voice. "Where is she? What happened?"

"Oh, goodness no," I said. "Nothing's happened. I was in a wreck with my car, and she came to my aid. Sweet girl, so caring. She's waiting with my car, talking to the police now. She was concerned you would be worried about her if she didn't appear when you arrived, so I said I would come over and fetch you."

He looked at me, suspicious but engaged. Mention of the police seemed to have settled him a bit. The illusion of security in helping professionals.

"Here, come this way," I said.

He came. We walked around the back of the school to a generous green space. It was a wooded park about two city blocks in size, separating the school from the downtown business district.

"Where are we going?" he said as I led him onto a path that disappeared into the trees.

"Oh it's just over by the old bookshop," I said. "It's quicker to cut through here."

He relaxed again. I recalled the armful of books that she had been carrying as she meandered out into the school yard, and figured that a trip to the bookstore would be a believable tale to spin to keep him moving forward to privacy.

"That kid and her books," he said, shaking his head. "She shouldn't be going off on her own like that, especially downtown."

"Yeah, I have two of my own," I nodded in agreement. We were bonding, and he was sufficiently lulled into a false sense of security. The element of surprise was crucial.

Once we were deeply entwined within the cover of the pines and poplars, I turned and veered off the paved path to a slightly less-beaten one, pushing us deeper into tree cover. No matter. No one shared the path with us today.

"I don't understand," he said, once we were standing deep in the tiny forest, where the shade from the trees made it feel like late dusk rather than high noon. "Where are we going?"

"We're here," I said, turning to him.

He stopped, and I swear I could see the pulse in his neck cease to throb. He realized something was off. *Strike now, Bruce.*

"She looked at me cock-eyed, that little trollop," I said with a sneer. "I hate little sluts like that, just coming into their own, thinking the siren song of their budding womanhood is an excuse for teasing and taunting us."

His fists balled.

"She'd never learn, you know. They never do, ones like her. Oh, the trouble she'd cause you! Much more than absconding to book stores. But I took care of it for you, buddy."

I reached around a wide poplar, and picked up my stash of triggers. I held out a handful of coppery ringlets, a book bag, and a bloody Converse running shoe.

"Didn't take much to coax her here, let me tell you. A pitiful story about needing help, and she followed me like an obedient little mutt. And obedient she remained, right until the end. I needed her to tell me about you, about who was coming for her, but she did that in a matter of seconds. Then I put her out of her misery. And the rest of the world, for having to endure her for a good eighty years or more."

He snapped like a dehydrated twig. I felt fists again, and every single bone in my body snapped and broke. His mournful howls echoed through the trees as my flesh was clawed and bit off my bones. The final blow was the forceful, jarring twist of my head being spun clear around until I could look straight down at my own ass. I stayed as still as I could while the man mewled and sobbed, convulsing on the ground. Finally he got up and loped towards the main road, pleading and crying and screaming for help.

I didn't kill her, of course. Even the blood on the shoe was mine from my still leaking nose. I'm not a monster. I simply gave her enough cash to get what I needed, enough to send him over the edge. In good time, they would forget all of this and go on living. No harm, no foul. For me, however, a million pound weight was lifted from my shoulders. The knots in my stomach loosened and untied, and the ache in my muscles subsided. I was refreshed, reborn. Pity it had to be at the expense of their emotional turmoil, but I was short on time. I really shouldn't have left it as long as I did. I vowed to be more proactive the next time, and catch the craving before it caught me.

I stood, brushed the debris of the forest floor off my clothes, and twisted my head back around to a forward-facing position. After a few minutes of aggressive yoga, my bones were set back in place, and my body appeared half-normal. A good shower and nap would took care of the rest. Then I went about my business, carrying on like a normal, average, boring fuck, until the need to be killed crept up on me again.

FLIGHT OF THE CROW

The hair around her face fanned out, gossamer butterfly wings shredded in webs on the glistening asphalt. The silver and black strands glistened like crystal in the morning sunlight. Warmth permeated the skin on her cheeks, skin damp from dew and pocked from the harsh sidewalk. She smiled.

The air was thick with humidity and a plethora of smells confirming the existence of humanity: food, fuel, waste, sweat. She breathed deep, reaching beyond the offensive—which always bullied the soft and delicate aromas out of the way—and smelled beauty. Shampoo, hydrangea, freshly baked pastries, morning coffee from the barista on the corner, the ocean. Even the scent of greasy street meat made her heart flutter.

"Yummy place, this world," she said to no one in particular.

Sister Crow rolled onto her knees, her bones and joints complaining even under her waifish frame. She rose to her feet, gathered and folded her blanket, and placed it gingerly in her cart as if it were a swaddled infant. She kissed her hand and lay it upon the soft pink fabric.

"Good mornin', love," she said, batting her eyes at the worn, stained fleece. She'd had the blanket for quite some time—ten years, give or take—and to her it was as precious as a diamond. And so much more beautiful.

She shuffled down the busy sidewalk, making eye contact with dozens of sets of eyes that refused to latch onto her longing gaze. She walked across the street and made her way past the ferry terminal and down onto the path along the sea wall. Once she had found a little nook to park her cart, she plucked Ol' Pinky out and set her on the ground, still folded. She sat on the blanket, and the gentle fleece cupped the boney curve of her wasting buttocks.

"Thank you, old friend," she said to the blanket.

Then she watched. People passed, they looked but didn't see; they raced and dashed and flitted about. And she watched. She watched their routines, their hopes, their drive, their pain. And felt it all. Then watched some more.

"It was never yours and never will be," a shrill voice whined in her ear.

Sister Crow swatted at her shoulder, her face deteriorating to a sullen gloom.

"Be gone, vile thing," Sister Crow growled.

People passing by gawked covertly from their peripherals, for fear acknowledgment might make Sister Crow's plight spread to their own grey matter like wildfire.

"All of that," the voice continued. "All the sensations, the purpose, the meaning. You've never had that in your life. And it's too late for you now. You're just an old bag of bones that's accomplished absolutely nothing."

"Shoo now," Sister Crow said firmly, a mother's scolding wrapped in a fearful whisper.

"You are a washed up, has-been, ne'er do good. And your expiration date is nigh, old crone. I know you feel it. I can smell the stench of your defeat."

Sister Crow drew a steady breath in through her nostrils, then exhaled through forcibly relaxed lips. She turned her head to the side, and locked onto two ruby-red orbs, each divided by a slit of obsidian. Dharius had been with her a long time, longer than she cared to remember, parroting the tongues of all her critics, including herself. She kept telling herself that she was stronger than the lies and hatred he spewed. Stronger than suggestions intended to keep her on her knees. He could chatter, but it would never sink so deep as to penetrate her heart. But sometimes...

"Resist me, crone," Dharius said, "but you know it to be true. You'll die a worthless sack of meat, leaving a mark on the world as inconsequential as the strike of a wet match. Useless. Pointless. An absolute waste—"

A slap sliced the words from Dharius's mouth. A tiny barbed tail, iridescent and glowing with remnants of moonlight, snapped around the back of Sister Crow's neck and struck Dharius across his black lips. He gasped in horror, then retreated down Sister Crow's sleeve, crumpled mewls escaping his bloodied jowls.

"Just in time," Sister Crow said, shuddering off the residual discomfort of Dharius's words. "He was on the verge of annoying me on this fine day."

Sister Crow looked to her left shoulder, where the faerie had perched. Its opalescent eyes glimmered in the sunlight and its lips were pursed in a soft smile. The silver faerie twirled Sister Crow's mangled hair through her delicate fingers, replacing knots with intricate braids just three strands thick. Sister Crow smiled, her heart swelling at the sight of the ethereal little creature. Hair like fire, skin a cold diamond-silver, solid black eyes, and plump ruby lips. She had no name, this faerie companion of hers... or maybe it did. The faerie had never uttered a single word in all the time Sister Crow had the pleasure of her friendship. The faerie simply kept Sister Crow company, touching her skin and her soul as the need for tenderness arose. And above all, she illuminated the beauty of the world.

Zara Mickelson hated the taste of her own blood.

She brought a tissue to her lips, avoiding eye contact with the mess in the mirror.

"Why today?" she asked the trembling reflection.

After dabbing the blood from her face, she addressed her appearance best as she could, spackling on layers of foundation and lipstick to mask the morning's activities. Once she looked like an undercover rodeo clown, she slipped on her blouse and headed downstairs to the kitchen.

"You okay?" Brent asked, his eyes studying the cream-to-caffeine ratio of his coffee.

"Sure," she said, delving right into her morning routine. Coffee, breakfast, pack bag, go. Go. Go.

"What's the rush?" he asked, his eyes abandoning cowardice and leaving his cup.

Go, go, go.

"Meeting this morning with the board. We're trying to get funding— "

"You have time to sit and eat with me," he said, tapping the table with a meaty finger.

"I really can't." Her voice quavered beneath a veil of assertion. "After we... I'm already later than I'd like to be."

He sighed.

That sigh.

I'll pay for this later, she thought as she scooped up her things and walked out the front door, leaving all hope of coffee, breakfast, and peace behind.

As Zara walked down the sidewalk to her office, her legs were cement, weighing her down as she tried to traverse the quicksand of life. *Everyone will see,* she thought as she brought her fingers to her throbbing lip.

Everyone will know.

She passed by street vendors and a plethora of pedestrians, blank faces moving along a slate-grey backdrop. *The world is an ugly place,* she thought. Her body was present, trudging towards her professional obligations, but her mind was still at home, gasping for air, drowning in a cyclonic tyranny of authority and domination. Every set of expressionless eyes that fell upon her face reminded her of her weakness, of the apathy of the world around her, and of her constant uphill battle. She moved through each day driven only by the second hand that pushed her tick by tock to the end, whatever end, *any* end that might bring the futility to conclusion.

Her stomach growled, startling her out of her inner frenzy. She realized that in her haste to escape, she hadn't eaten breakfast. She certainly couldn't add hangry to her myriad of emotions, so she stopped at a street-meat vendor, selecting a spicy breakfast taco she could consume quickly before work. Once the greasy fare was in hand, she wandered across the street, drawn by the gentle waves of the ocean. She walked along the inner seawall, plunked herself down on a bench, and took a bite. The generous helping of hot sauce seeped from the edges of the taco, dribbling down her stinging lip and onto the front of her cream-colored blouse. She looked at the bright orange spot, but her eyes trailed to the surrounding droplets. Minuscule splotches of browning crimson, smattered over the front of her shirt. *Blood*, she thought.

And she cried.

Sister Crow watched the worn and deflated woman stop to indulge in a mobile breakfast before the devastating spill on that fateful park bench. She observed in fascination as the little dribble of pulverized pepper sauce drew an unnecessary amount of tears.

"Spicy, but not sad," Sister Crow whispered to herself. "Spicy is not sad, is it?" she asked the silver faerie on her shoulder.

The faerie twittered with excitement, bouncing and cartwheeling down Sister Crow's arm and into her lap, a trail of light flowing behind her like a bridal train made of Christmas tinsel.

"What has your knickers in a knot?" Sister Crow asked the faerie, then looked back at the woman on the bench. The woman was still crying, hot sauce on her face and despair slumping her frail body. "I've no time for your energy right now," Sister Crow said, brushing the faerie to the side. "I gotta tend to this missus." The faerie dissolved into glitter, swirling away with the wind like a sparkling dust devil.

Sister Crow started towards the bench, but stopped short when she got a better look at the woman's face.

"Ah," Sister Crow said, her eyes dimming. She examined the woman from head to toe: her professional attire, fingernails gnawed and picked straight to the quick, the nervous tap of her bargain-basement heels. Sister Crow proceeded to the bench and sat next to the weeping wanderer, so close that their outer thighs touched.

ZARA STARTLED at the sudden and unwanted guest who evidently had zero respect for personal space.

"'Tis only a bit o' sauce," the old woman said.

The woman had long, straggly salt-and-pepper hair, skin marked with the roadmap of a laborious life, and a tattered old gown meant only for covering the unmentionables. Zara recoiled at the sight of her, but something in that woman's eyes kept Zara's ass planted firmly on that bench.

"I'm sorry?" Zara said, leaning back but not sliding over.

"Sauce, dear," Sister Crow said, pointing at the hot sauce on Zara's blouse. "And blood, too, but nobody be noticin' that against that fluorescent pepper sludge. Your spill is a blessin', methinks, if you were trying to draw attention from that lip o' yours."

Sister Crow brought her bony digit up to Zara's face. Zara flinched and then lowered her eyes to the worn toes of her shoes. Sister Crow withdrew her hand, folding it with the other on her lap.

"Nah," Sister Crow said, her brow furrowed to a fat caterpillar. "Ashamed is foolish. You? You had nothing to do with that mess. I'd wear that like a badge o' honor. It tells the world you have survived dealings with a cowardly idiot."

Zara's tears turned to giggles despite the funk that shrouded her heart. Sister Crow smiled and raised her hand in the air.

"Now, child," Sister Crow said. "I'm gonna place my hand on yours, and I'm gonna hold it. And you're gonna let me."

Zara didn't have time to argue. Midblink and halfway through a startled inhalation, Sister Crow's hand was around hers, clasping it as a grandmother would. And Zara did exactly what Sister Crow directed. She let her. She didn't pull back, she didn't resist. What she did do, however, was like it.

SISTER CROW ENJOYED the extended company her new friend gave her. A long overdue dose of human contact, both physical and emotional.

One hour.

For one hour, the women sat on that bench, hands held tight, conversation sporadic, breathing in the sea air as they took in the world around them.

"How are you... where you are?" Zara asked, her eyes dipping to her feet.

"Confidence, child," Sister Crow scolded. "Speak your thoughts with assertion. Your curiosity is harmless, and your thoughts are your right."

Zara nodded, drawing a deep breath and trying again. "Why are you homeless? Who are you?"

"Sister Crow," she said, her mouth drawing into a tight line. "The kids, they all call me that because o' my treasures." Sister Crow nodded back towards the shopping cart nestled in an overgrown corner of the boardwalk. "I love the world and all its beauty. The discarded lipstick tubes, the foil wrappers, the coins, the hair." Sister crow shrugged her shoulders. "A crow, you see."

Zara nodded.

"Garbage, though," Zara mumbled, taking care to keep her eyes elevated.

"Life," Sister Crow retorted. "It's all life."

"No, she's right," Dharius hissed in Sister Crow's ear. "Garbage. You, your life, everything you've done, or rather failed to do."

Sister Crow jolted, swatting at her shoulder and muttering profanities to the empty air.

"You disgust her," Dharius continued. "You are so far beneath anyone and anything, you filthy sow."

"Shut it, you bugger," Sister Crow groaned.

Zara furrowed her brow, looking across Sister Crow to the offending patch of nothing above her shoulder.

Cue the faerie, who quickly put an end to the debasement, using her flaming red hair to bind and gag Dharius and throw him to the ground. The little demon writhed and contorted, the faerie's crimson tresses flowing out of his ears and nose as she dominated him. Sister Crow looked at the pinned devil, and the silver faerie sitting cross-legged on his belly, its silver head bobbing to some catchy tune within its own skull. Sister Crow looked back over at Zara, whose face had gone from pink-tinged ivory to ashen grey.

"Ah, sorry," Sister Crow said. "Schizophrenia."

Zara said nothing. She reached out and took Sister's Crow's hand, letting their intertwined fingers rest once again across their thighs. The sparkle of a tear swelled across Sister Crow's vision, glistening off the silver flesh of her faerie. She let the tear trickle down her wrinkled cheek. *Emotion is so beautiful and powerful,* she thought, making no move to hide her tear.

"So why are *you* here?" Sister Crow asked.

"I work down the street in the old Strathcona building."

"Boring," Sister Crow snipped. "I mean, why are you in this place in your life? How did you become this defeated slip of a woman, blind to the beauty of life, skulking through your day looking for an end like a character in a side-scrolling video game?"

Zara gasped, offended. She opened her mouth to argue, to quip a retort, but remained silent. She had been hit by the truth, but not blindsided by it. She turned her head and faced the sea. The whisper of the waves rolling against the pier filled her ears, accentuated by the song of gulls seeking treasures the likes of which Sister Crow would covet. She pictured those gulls flying across the sea to distant shores, free of the dust of this life; free of hurt and pain, doubt and worry.

"Sometimes I wish I could fly," Zara said. "Take to the wind, cross the bay, and start anew. Let my journey across the sea cleanse the rottenness that blinds me and the sludge that weighs me down. Lighten my wings and clear my mind."

Despite her new awareness of her own submissive posturing, Zara allowed her eyes to examine her shoes once again. "But I fear that even if I did, nothing would change. Or it would change for the worse. I am who I am, and that's something I cannot go back from."

Sister Crow sat in quiet contemplation for a moment before placing her other hand on Zara's back.

"I wish you could see yourself through my eyes," Sister Crow said.

"You don't know me," Zara said, her brief euphoria of escapism dissipating.

"I know you," Sister Crow said. "I refuse to wallow, so I see things, notice things. I am so little and have so little," Sister Crow winced, and glanced down at the venomous demon tethered to the concrete, "that I find beauty in less."

Zara's cellphone shouted at her. She dropped Sister Crow's hand and pulled the vibrating social tether from her pocket.

"Oh shit," Zara grumbled. "I'm late."

She looked towards Sister Crow without really seeing her and dashed from the bench.

"It was nice meeting you," Zara called back over her shoulder as she sprinted back up to the street.

Sister Crow grimaced as her new friend became blind once again.

IT SHOULD BE OKAY, right?

I nailed the presentation. I deserve a celebration. So this is fine, right?

Zara worried her fingers through the tips of her hair, twitching at each and every little noise: the clink of a glass, an explosion of laughter, the bang of a pint set down on a heavy wooden table.

The day had gone well. So well, in fact, that her coworkers had insisted they all go out for celebratory beverages at the pub around the corner. Zara had begrudgingly obliged. A part of her, hidden way down at the tip of her pinky toe, enjoyed the revelry, the social interaction, the camaraderie. But the majority of her buckled in fear, knowing the impending consequences for her blatant change in routine.

She had called him, several times, but he often left his phone in another room or in a coat pocket. She hadn't come home after work, and her plans had not been previously discussed. And now she was late. Very late. And her phone was dead.

And so am I, she thought.

She feigned interest in the conversations filling the stale pub air, wanting so badly to fit in, to enjoy herself, to forget the reality lurking beyond the pub doors. Out in the night, another world waited for her behind a door a mere twenty blocks from where she sat; it was a world filled with tears, fists, blood, and a vicious tongue. She wrung her hands together beneath the table, attempting to massage her nagging anxiety into submission. She could still feel her, Sister Crow, the firmness of her grasp and her beautiful outlook on life. Zara closed her eyes and pictured Sister Crow's face, the brightness in her eyes, the colors of the world gravitating to her happiness.

Zara smiled and took a sip of her drink.

ONE DRINK TURNED TO MANY, sitting rose to dancing, and conversation lifted to song and raucous laughter. As one day stumbled into the next, the herd thinned, leaving Zara and a few stragglers to be flushed out into the night come closing time. The remainder of her crew boarded the metro or taxis, but Zara opted to hoof it home. She needed fresh air and time to clear her head before entering the den of the beast.

"You sure you don't want to jump in? We can easily swing by your place. No trouble at all."

Scott, the effeminate IT support guy with his red hair and pale skin, was anything but threatening, and was certainly soothing, but she needed the walk to get herself together.

"No, thanks, Scott," she said,

"You know..." Scott said, his voice trailing off.

Zara noticed his eyes flicker briefly to her swollen lip, and pity flavored his expression. Her eyes sought her shoes for solace as she waved her hand dismissively in his direction.

"Goodnight, Scott."

He paused, giving her one last look before his taxi whisked him away into the night.

Zara walked down the street, retracing her steps to the boardwalk where she had sat with Sister Crow in the morning sun, staring out over the ocean. She slowed at their bench, pausing to look out over the glassy water. She thought of Sister Crow and of the distant shores that haunted her desires.

"Who is he?"

Zara spun around and was caught off guard by an explosive looking Brent, his fists balled and face red.

"Brent, I—"

"You what? Are screwing around on me with that *ginger*?"

She looked at the bench, then directly into Brent's eyes.

"I went out for drinks. After work. We had a good day, we nailed the contract, and we went out to celebrate."

She stood tall. She did not look at her feet.

"I tried to call," she explained.

Sweat beaded on his brow.

"I'm sorry, sweetheart," Zara sighed.

Then, for the second time during those waking hours, Zara tasted her own blood.

"No!" Sister Crow yelped in a stifled scream.

She peered from her hidey-hole as the brute put his hands on her beautiful, damaged friend. As he forcefully exerted his perceived entitlement, Sister Crow turned her head to look away.

"You were nothing to her, anyway," Dharius whispered, licking the inside of her ear with his forked tongue. "You are just a slob, a waste of human flesh taking up real estate on a planet meant for beings with purpose."

The faerie lashed out, attempting to silence the micro-devil with a slash of her tail, but he put up a fight. He wrapped his tiny red talons around her silver neck. She responded by thrusting her golden tongue down his throat, protecting Sister Crow from his wretched commentary. Sister Crow watched as the little folks fought, silvery skin chaffing against black, leathery scales, both sets of eyes glowing with passionate determination. The faerie could have overcome the little devil, but instead, she thrust out a silvery finger, casting a crystalized light towards the sparring couple. Sister Crow's eyes followed the trail of light, her vision reaching the scene the very moment Zara was mid-fall. In slow motion, with the little devil cheering and taunting through what sounded like an ocean of molasses, Zara's head struck the bench where they had sat, where they had held hands, and where the world had stopped for a spell. And now that world was still and quiet, save the sound of the whispering waves and thump of Sister's Crow's breaking heart.

Sister Crow didn't hesitate. She loped down the seawall, brandishing little more than Ol' Pinky as a weapon, pushing forward until the palms of her wise and weathered hands met the brute's chest.

"You pig!" she screamed. "You pathetic coward!"

She pounded his chest and clawed at his face, tearing flesh wherever her nails caught purchase. Her hair flailed around her head like the manic snakes of Medusa, and spittle flew from her chapped lips. She became more beast than woman, more volatile than her personal little devil, but she was no match for a male so many years her junior. She felt it, every punch of his fist, every kick of his boot. As her head came to rest on the salty pavement, she couldn't help but wonder at how beautiful the stars were in the night sky.

THE STARS WERE STILL THERE when Sister Crow opened her eyes. They were still shone brightly, the moon still high in the sky.

"Hrmph," she groaned. "Mus' still be nighttime."

She didn't know how long she had been out, but it couldn't have been too great a time if the night was in full bloom. The bastard had pummeled her after 2am, and the sun's alarm rang at 6, so she was somewhere in between. She turned her head and saw Zara laying face-down in front of the bench, a pool of blood formed beneath the stream trickling from her lips. Zara's chest heaved, slightly and slowly, but enough to show she still drew breath.

"Good girl. Stay strong."

Sister Crow used her hands to grope her own body, searching for what might be out of place and waiting to hinder her effort. *Everything,* she concluded, pangs of pain shot through her broken body, and there were spears of bone where bone should not have been. "Ah well. I was becomin' obsolete, anyway." *That one, though...* she thought, looking over at Zara.

Using every ounce of fortitude in her mind, body, and soul, Sister Crow struggled to her knees, then to her haunches, and finally hoisted herself to her feet. She walked over to the bench and cringed as she dropped back down to the ground.

"Girl, I'm gonna touch you, okay?"

Sister Crow ran her hands along Zara's body, relieved to find she was relatively intact. Aside from a likely concussion, the brute had inflicted some superficial bruising and emotional heartache, but not much more. Sister Crow got to her feet again and walked to her cart. The faerie was perched in a nearby tree, still and silent, breathless in anticipation.

"Okay, little one. Let's get to work."

RED KISSED THE MORNING SKY, casting a pink glow over the lazy fog lingering over the water. Zara woke to pain and confusion. Her vision was milky, and her tongue pasty and dry. Her head pounded a dull, steady waltz.

Brent.

She sat up and pressed her hand against her chest, sighing in relief at the beat against her palm.

Okay. I'm alive.

She touched her head and found one hell of a goose egg perched on her temple. Her body ached, and she cringed against abrasions on her knees and arms. Thankfully, someone had covered her in a pink blanket that sheltered her from the crisp sea air. She pulled off the blanket and looked down at her blouse, expecting additional blood on the already stained outfit. There was more blood, yes, and a lot of it. But over the blood, fastened to her blouse by safety pins and scotch tape, were pieces of garbage—flyers, wrappers, discarded scraps of fabric, feathers—cut into all manner of shapes. Hearts, stars, snowflakes. She stared at the adorn-ments, seeing them more as decorations than garbage. Shiny foil, vibrant colors, precisely constructed art. And her skin, pallid ivory, bruised and tainted, was scripted with dozens of messages scrawled in paint and food and fluids of question-able origins.

You are beautiful.

You are more than this.

You are not trapped.

You are powerful

You belong only to yourself.

You are a part of the world, and you have use. Beauty. Emotion. Purpose.

Be you.

Be free.

Fly.

Zara frantically scanned the area, and she saw it, in a nook tucked away at the end of the boardwalk behind a bush ripe with flowers. Feet, bloodied and contorted at unnatural angles, peeking out from behind their floral blind.

"Oh!" Zara exclaimed.

She stood, her legs realizing they must carry her weight. She hobbled over to the bush and swiped away the brambles, revealing her now-broken friend.

"Sister Crow," Zara said, tears spilling from her swollen eyes.

Sister Crow tried to sit up, but her body wouldn't comply, leaving her limp and sputtering on the ground.

"Ah, it's no odds, child," Sister Crow sputtered as she raised a hand to Zara's cheek.

Zara fumbled for her pockets then glanced at the bench where her purse lay. She moved to stand, but Sister Crow stopped her and clasped her hand against her breast.

"Let me call an ambulance," Zara pleaded. "The police."

"It's my end, child," Sister Crow said, a weak smile on her

face. "He done me good. But it's my time. I have no fear or regret. Life has been good and beautiful and kind. And long enough."

Sister Crow's eyes drifted from Zara's face, following the glowing light over her shoulder. The faerie was there, a beacon against the backdrop of crimson sky, her gleaming, glittering skin sending the rising sun pirouetting in lyrical prisms.

"He did this," Zara said on feeble breath.

"He did," Sister Crow said, smiling despite the pain.

"You tried to stop him. To save me."

"I did."

They were quiet. They held hands and smiled until the bustle of routine ignited on the street behind the boardwalk.

"I can't leave you here like this," Zara whispered, her lower lip quavering.

"You can, and you will," Sister Crow said, smiling something just over Zara's shoulder. "Don't worry. I'm not alone."

Zara let herself cry, moistening her friend in a heartfelt tear-bath that cleansed them both. Zara pried Sister Crow's hand from hers and retrieved Ol' Pinky from the bench. She returned the blanket to Sister Crow, drawing it over her battered body and up to her chin. Sister Crow squealed and hugged into the blanket, nuzzling her face into its familiar embrace.

Zara went to stand, and Sister Crow grabbed her arm.

"And what of you?" Sister Crow asked, and the faerie's glow faded, waiting for the answer.

Zara thought, though the decision had already cemented itself in her heart. She looked at her body, the beautiful disaster of garbage, the messages of love and hope, and turned her eyes to the sea.

"Good," Sister Crow said. "Very good, then."

"But he can't get away with this," Zara said.

"He won't," Sister Crow said. "It will weigh on him, the viciousness, his loss. It will eat him like a bucket of maggots wedged into his guts."

Zara looked unsure.

"That," Sister Crow said, a wicked smile stretching her lips, "and I got a piece o' him. A wee souvenir for the cops when they find me."

She held up her hand, and Zara saw that her long nails were bloodied, strips of flesh and clumps of hair embedded deep under her yellowed claws. And, most importantly, the tattered leather wallet clutched in Sister Crow's bony grasp.

Zara smiled.

She knelt down and kissed the old woman on the forehead, and they held each other's faces for a long moment before Zara walked away.

SISTER CROW WATCHED as the no-longer defeated woman walked away. She watched as a ticket was purchased and those scuffed shoes left the dock.

"Good," Sister Crow said, heavy sobs creeping out between shallow breaths.

Sister Crow felt a soft hand against her cheek. The faerie was there, stroking her skin, bright aqua tears of joy twinkling in her crystal eyes. Sister Crow looked from side to side, seeking the faerie's adversary, but Dharius was nowhere to be found.

The faerie extended a long, floating finger and tapped Sister Crow on the chest. For the first time ever, the faerie opened her mouth and spoke. The word was musical, a beautiful note that resonated clear through to Sister Crow's soul.

"*Hero.*"

The world crumbled into a kaleidoscope of color, then faded to silver, brighter, brighter...

And Sister Crow smiled.

ZARA IMAGINED Sister Crow's hand. She felt it upon her own as she purchased her ticket to board the ferry, as she stepped aboard the empty boat, and as she pulled away from shore, heading to the great unknown. She could feel her friend's hand upon her face as she looked up at the sky, the warmth of the sun soothing her healing skin. Zara had nothing, but she had everything. She had no belongings, no immediate plans; she had nothing but the clothes on her back and the purse on her arm. But she had hope. She had a future.

She had a new start.

She walked to the bow of the boat and gazed out across the open water, imagining her first step on her next shore. She closed her eyes.

And she flew.

THE MAN WITH THE RED OCTOPUS BALLOON

It had been a long day, a long day indeed, Melvin thought as he boarded the Number 48, destined for his home in Rapier Heights where his wife would be waiting with a Merlot and some Chinese takeaway. He and Carol would sit down with those little cardboard containers and their stemless wineglasses and watch some indie horror movies on Netflix.

Melvin adored Fridays.

What he did not adore, however, was the stench of that old bus.

Urine, diesel fuel, mint chewing gum, and body odour, with undertones of beef and onion.

On this particular Friday, the bus was packed with people and their smells. Melvin stood, grasping the greasy overhead bar to minimize his contact with the surrounding steerage.

But not even the stench or filth could dampen his glow. It was Friday. And Melvin adored Fridays.

As bus swayed, Melvin thought of his wife—her silver hair, the bright red lipstick on her lips, the giggle as she sipped her wine. They still felt and acted like teenagers, hearts and stomachs a flutter and their souls ripe with life.

Oh, how Melvin wished the bus would hurry up and carry him home to his Friday night with Carol.

As he looked ahead, counting the number of people and calculating the potential number of stops, something caught his eye. A red balloon bounced off the ceiling every time they struck a pothole or bump on the road. It was lovely. A child's prized possession downtown, he supposed.

Stop after stop, minute after minute, people stepped off, one at a time, two at a time, carrying briefcases and parcels, purses and umbrellas, until the bus was practically empty. Melvin was in all his glee, still on his feet, too excited to sit and be still for the last moments of the ride. He looked out the windshield towards his destination, but his eyes drifted to the ceiling. To the red balloon.

Melvin and the owner of the red balloon were the only two left on the bus. He couldn't see the person with the balloon, who was hunched over in their seat. Melvin craned his neck to see the hand at the end of the balloon string.

He walked forward, stepping gingerly so as not to lose his balance, and took the seat opposite the owner of the red balloon.

"Hello there," Melvin said, tipping his hat.

"Hello," the man said. He was reading a book. The balloon was tied to his wrist.

"Mighty fine balloon you've got there," Melvin said.

"Why thank you," the balloon owner said, not looking up from his book.

"It's just... I thought you were a child. The balloon and all."

The man with the balloon lifted his head, his eyes black and stormy, sunken deep in his face. His head was bald and shiny. His teeth were large and dull; he bared them when he spoke.

"Now, why would I be a child? Are balloons reserved for the children alone?"

"Well, no, but it's unusual—"

"What if I had a child, waiting for me at home, a birthday or afternoon treat or the like?"

"Perhaps, yes. I apologize. I meant no offense."

"None taken, of course." The man with the balloon laughed. "I have no child, though. The balloon is for me."

"For you?" Melvin asked, tilting his head.

"For me, yes. A celebration."

"Well, a celebration! Congratulations! And what are you celebrating?"

"Change," the man with the balloon said. He looked up at the balloon. As did Melvin. It was then that Melvin realized it was an...

"Octopus," the man said, a giggle in his voice. "Isn't it positively ridiculous?"

"Well, I'll be damned," Melvin said, stroking his chin and looking up at the odd shaped balloon. "I do say, I've never seen an octopus balloon, red or otherwise."

"It's unusual, that's for sure. That's why I chose this for my celebration."

"Because it's unusual?"

"Because it's not normal. Not expected. People need to embrace change, to want the unknown."

"Oh?" Melvin said.

"Monotony is cement, bogging us down and dragging us towards our death."

The balloon owner's expression hardened, his dark gaze boring into Melvin's brain. Melvin shifted in his seat and tugged at his tie.

"Tell me, good sir," the man with the balloon said as he twirled his fingers around the balloon string, "is your life expected? Is it normal?"

Melvin held the man's stare, his heart fluttering, his bowels clenching.

"Why yes, my life is normal, but—"

"For how long?"

"Excuse me? I—"

"How long has it been normal? Expected? Predictable?"

"I'll have you know I like my life the way it is. Love it, in fact."

"It is mind numbing, yes?"

"It is peaceful," Melvin argued, his face flushing with anger. "And I say, you shan't judge me, sir. You know nothing of my life and my happiness. Good day to you, then."

Melvin stood and walked to the front of the bus to wait for his stop. He was still excited to see his Carol, to sip that wine and eat Chinese food, but a cloud hung over him now. *How dare that man be so rude.* He clucked his tongue. *He doesn't know. He doesn't know me and mine.*

He looked in the reflection of the window a few times, watching the man. The red balloon bobbed and danced every time he turned a page in his book. The man didn't say anything more, didn't lift his head, nothing. *How dare he, after being so rude.*

By the time the bus pulled up to Melvin's stop, he was in a tizzy. The bus doors squealed open, but Melvin heard another sound. A low, rumbling rasp. He looked back at the man with the red balloon. The man was laughing, his mouth opening wider and the sound growing louder with each passing second. It was a braying, honking gasp of a chortle. The red octopus balloon flailed as if having a fit.

And then the man was gone, vanished before his eyes, like he had never been there at all.

Melvin stumbled off the bus, then took off in a jog. His heart pounding in his chest and tears swelled in his eyes. *Melvin, calm yourself. Don't let that riff raff crawl under your skin. It's Friday. And you adore Fridays. Wine. Food. Carol.*

Melvin burst through the front door of his house, slamming it behind him and snapping the lock closed. And the chain for good measure.

He and Carol never used the chain.

"Carol!" he called out, a massive quaver marring the excitement that should have been in his voice. "Carol, I'm home! The damnedest thing just happened, Lord help me..."

Melvin kicked off his shoes, a sense of relief washing over him as the smells and lights of his life warmed his soul. He breathed in deep, the smell of Carol's nutmeg incense filling his nostrils.

He stopped.

"Carol?"

There was no Chinese takeaway. He should have smelled the orange chicken and ginger beef. Certainly the spicy aroma of the beef.

He hustled to the kitchen, expecting to find paper boxes and foil containers lining the island, but it was bare.

"Carol! Where are you, Carol?"

He rubbed his hand, longing for the brush of her finger as she handed him his glass of wine.

The corkscrew was still in its holder and the wine was still in the rack.

"Carol!"

Melvin became frantic—running from room to room, calling her name, opening every door, and turning over every blanket and pillow and paper. When he reached the master bedroom, he was out of breath, panic clutching at his throat.

"Carol?"

A lavender slip of paper sat atop their navy bedclothes, crinkled and left in a ball. Melvin stared at it for a moment then fetched it, smoothing it out in his tired old hands.

Congratulations, Melvin and Carol, on your decision to make Eden's Landing your retirement home! Thank you for submitting all the paperwork. Your move-in date will be Monday, August 21st. Your move-in details are included in your package...

WHAT? Leave our home?

Our furniture, our shows, our kitchen and that yellow half-bath we love so much?

Leave our Friday nights, our wine, our Chinese take away, our horror shows?

"Never!" he shouted.

Melvin crumpled the paper and threw it back down on the bed.

He stormed out of the bedroom, furious at Eden's Landing, at Carol, and the man with the red octopus ballon.

"Why does everything have to change?" Melvin yelled,

projecting his voice through the flat. "I won't stand for it, no I won't!"

He went to the kitchen, snatched a bottle of merlot from the rack, and slammed it down on the counter. "I'll get my own damn wine, thank you very much."

He grabbed the cork screw and jammed it in the cork, a little too forcefully, as it turned out. The wine bottle shattered in his hand, bathing him in glass and crimson merlot.

Melvin stood there, staring at the puddle on the floor, at the stains on his clothes, at his hands dripping with red. He brushed at his slacks, but the red simply spread, thick and tacky and dark.

This isn't wine at all. I've cut myself, I have.

Rinsing his hands in the sink, he doused a dishtowel and dabbed at his shirt and pants. The blood had soaked in, covering his chest and the front of his trousers in a large, sopping stain.

Oh, I've really done a number, haven't I?

He washed his hands a second time then went to the master bath to remove his shirt and pants. Standing in front of the mirror in his thin, white briefs, he examined his grey, sagging body. Pale and clean. No blood.

"But I..."

No cuts. Only smears of blood that had seeped through his clothing.

Slow motion, one deliberate step at a time, he wandered back to the kitchen. The wine bottle was smashed, but the bottom half sat neatly, as if it had been placed on the counter.

"Oh Carol! Oh..."

Carol lay on the floor in a pool of blood, her neck opened from ear to ear, lavender papers still crumpled in her fist.

"No, no, no..."

He remembered.

He remembered the talk they'd had. The argument. All the arguments over many months.

They needed to move. For his health.

His dementia.

And the red balloon she had bought him as a gift. For the move.

Melvin looked down at his body, at the neck of the wine bottle still clutched in his hand.

And he looked at his beloved Carol, her beautiful brown eyes wide and fixed, her lips painted red and cheeks pallid and waxy.

And there was the red octopus balloon, floating in the air, tied to her wrist...

THE ESCAPE

"*R*un, Clara! Now!"

Paula watched her youngest cowering beneath the picnic table, clutching onto her stuffed bear for dear life. Barely more than a slip of a thing, Clara's wispy blonde hair was blowing in the breeze, her big blue eyes overflowing with tears. She was in the middle of the campsite, only about ten meters away, but to the young girl it must have felt like a hundred kilometers.

"Ethan, you have to go get her," Paula shouted at her husband in a whisper.

Ethan looked panicked. Paula's two older children hung on him, one on each arm, all three crouched behind the cover of a huge oak. Paula scanned the trees, rustling doom in the windy day. She was unable to detect any foreign movement mixed in with the mass of branches and leaves blowing in the breeze. All the sounds were muddled together with the crashing from the nearby falls.

Paula wasn't going to sit idly by and watch them take her daughter. Taking a deep breath, she lunged from her hidey hole behind a fallen log. She crossed the campsite in three long lopes and rolled under the table with Clara, grinding her knees in the gravel in the process. She rubbed her battered skin then embraced her daughter.

"It's okay, sweetie. Mom's here."

Clara nestled into Paula's bosom. Paula wrapped an arm around the shivering girl as they crawled out from under the table. No time to waste. No hesitating to cross the open expanse again.

They reached the others without incident.

"Thank fuck," Ethan said, wrapping his arms around his wife and youngest child. The other children joined in, squishing Clara and Paula together.

"Enough," Paula said, wriggling out of their grasp. "We need to move. Now."

Brian and Hannah grabbed the packs and Ethan scooped his gun up off the ground. Paula led the way, heading into the woods and away from the campground. Brian and Hannah kept to the middle of the pack, scanning the sides as they moved. Ethan brought up the rear, keeping every family member in his sight. Initially, they had travelled in opposite order, with Ethan and the gun leading the way. But once they realized they were being followed, not approached from the front, they switched positions.

Paula veered them away from the stream. Once, before it all went to shit, she would have loved the sound, the babbling water splashing against the rocks, the trickle of streams and small waterfalls cascading here and there. But now the rushing water was just a distraction, a hinderance to the detection of voices and footsteps. She wished the river dead and still.

THOUGH THEY HAD BEEN SPARED the full wrath of the midday sun by the grace of heavy tree cover, Paula was grateful for nightfall. She figured those hunting them would be less adept at moving through the woods at night. Not that Paula and her family were great at it, but they had been preparing. Practicing. And they were equipped with the tools to aid them in their journey: night vision goggles, mosquito nets, and dark clothing to help blend them into the midnight hour.

"Should we rest?" Ethan asked.

Paula glanced at her family, but was greeted by shadows, illusions and movements of deceit thrown by the light of the moon. *We're probably safe.* Agony wracked her gut as she considered how weary her children must be. Brian and Hannah were teenagers, but they were still kids. Her kids. She had a responsibility to keep them healthy and happy and safe.

"Yes," Paula said, slowing her feet.

"We passed a small flat spot back there," Ethan said. "We could throw down some blankets, and—"

"No," Paula said. "We don't go backwards. Always forwards. We'll push on until we come to another suitable spot."

Twenty minutes later, they came across a patch of forest where the trees were sparse and the ground barren enough to make camp. Brian and Hannah went to work, unrolling blankets and setting up in relative silence. Not speaking, barely breathing. Ethan stood sentry, infrared goggles strapped to his head and gun scope to his eye. He kept sweeping the woods in a circle, waiting, watching.

Paula was proud of him, staying so strong for all of them, especially for Clara. Clara lay sound asleep in Paula's arms, all cares forgotten as she dreamed, hopefully about her Care Bear blanket back at home and their golden retriever, Sally. Hopefully not about the last six months that had been stolen from her.

It would all be over soon.

The wind had decided to call it a night as well, quieting the forest to a gentle slumber. Paula felt relieved for the respite from the sounds of the river and the movements of the wind. The calm would make it much easier to detect anyone who might approach them while they rested.

"You sleep," Ethan said. "You've carried her all day. Get a few hours, then we'll switch out. I feel fine."

Paula nodded. She would have argued, tried to be stronger for her husband and her family, but she was tired, exhausted straight to the core. She walked over to Ethan, tilted her head around the goggles, and pressed her lips against his. He was warm and wet and tasted like home.

We'll get back there.

Mud and smoke.

Paula woke, her face pressed into the dirt, the taste of mud and smoke heavy on her tongue. She swallowed a few times, pushing her tongue around her mouth to summon some saliva and relive the tackiness. It occurred to her that she hadn't stopped to drink even once during their jaunt from the campsite, and dehydration was starting to set in.

The children possibly, too.

Red, warm light glowed through her eyelids. A new day was upon them.

Not much longer now, she thought. A glimmer of a smile tugged at the corners of her dry, cracked mouth.

She sat up and stretched, opening her eyes to the emerald shimmer of the morning forest. It was bright out, the sun having already crawled halfway up the sky. And the heat had dissolved any fog that might have been hanging over the lush foliage earlier in the day.

Like a sledgehammer, her heart thrust against the inside of her ribcage.

It was morning. Late morning.

Too late.

How fucking long were we asleep?

Paula shot to her feet and gave her eyes an aggressive swipe with the back of her hand to clear them into focus. Brian and Hannah here still sleeping, huddled together beneath a blanket at the foot of a large poplar. Other than that, the clearing was devoid of any signs of life. No Ethan. No Clara.

Simply throwing her hand over her mouth would not prevent her from calling out, from screaming her daughter's name. Paula ripped the bandana off her head and clenched it between her teeth, sobbing into the thick cotton to muffle the sound.

Focus, Paula. Look.

She scoured the ground, hunting for Ethan's footsteps, for evidence of Clara, for anything. Unfortunately, the wind was also awake, and had littered the ground with leaves and all manner of disrupted forest debris, unsettling any trail her missing family members might have left behind.

Where would they go?

They would go back where they came from.

Paula doubled back, following the trail towards the campsite. No one would take Clara and venture further away from civilization. She didn't have to go far before her instincts proved correct.

Ethan stood, night vision goggle hanging haphazardly around the back of his neck, gun to his eye, pointed down the trail. Paula approached with caution, peering over his shoulder at his target.

The target was a large man dressed head to toe in camouflage with a two-way radio in his hand and his other arm wrapped around a squirming, struggling Clara. Though she fought violently against his grasp, she remained silent, her lips pressed firmly together.

Good girl. Paula was proud of her daughter's commitment to silence, even when engulfed in fear.

Paula knew Ethan didn't want to shoot. He was stuck there in frightened hope that the man would just hand Clara back without a fight.

Paula made eye contact with the man and held there, communicating threats through a hard stare. He lifted the radio to his mouth. Paula shook her head. Ethan's finger caressed the trigger.

"Don't do it," Paula mouthed as clear as she could, hoping the stranger would catch her drift.

Either he didn't, or he didn't care.

His finger pressed the button on the two-way radio, silencing the soft static emanating from the tiny speaker.

He wasn't able to get a single word out before Ethan pulled the trigger. The stranger's head exploded, spraying the surrounding trees with gore. Paula lunged forward and ripped Clara out of his arms before the body slumped to the ground. Clara's little white dress with the pastel flowers was already covered in dirt, but now it was thick with meat, blood, and bone. Paula wiped at it, then started pulling fragments of bone from Clara's golden ringlets.

"We have to go," Ethan said, touching Paula's arm.

She knew that. They couldn't stop now, not until they got where they were going. That shot had blasted through the woods like a gong, telling everyone within a ten kilometer radius where they were.

By the time they arrived back at the clearing—a few minutes, at most—Brian and Hannah had packed up and were ready to go.

"We heard the shot," Hannah said, "and got ready as fast as we could."

"Great job, kids," Ethan said, patting Hannah's back and ruffling Brian's hair.

Brian took Clara from Paula and began picking globs of brain matter off her face.

The family moved quick and quiet, diverting towards the river. Paula figured that those following them wouldn't expect them to go close to the river because of the noise. But that didn't matter now. The shotgun blast would have sent them in the family's general direction. Speed was key now. They were almost there. They would make it.

It was dark by the time they reached their destination. Over the past few hours, they had been pushing their limits, keeping a steady pace just below a run. It had been hard on them, especially on the kids—who were hauling packs—and Ethan—who had taken Clara so Paula could lead the way through the thick brush. When they finally saw the towering sequoia, branches like long fingers reaching out to grab the trembling bipeds, all five were on the precipice of madness and exhaustion. Sounds all around threatened capture, the rustles of the leaves, the cawing of a crow. Everything raised Paula's hackles.

It had been a long spell of pain, of suffering, of physical attacks and screams of horror shredding their every waking moment.

Long enough.

"Lovie," she said, reaching for Clara.

But she's not. She's not my lovie anymore. Hasn't been for quite some time.

Clara nestled into her mom's chest and began winding Paula's hair through her fingers. Her other hand went to her face, thumb in mouth, eyes dipping lower, heavier, until they were slender slits barely glistening in the moonlight.

"C'mon now," Paula said, excitement in her voice. "Let's hurry."

The family launched into gear, each tackling their assigned tasks with methodical precision. Hannah and Brian unpacked the bags, laying the contents out in rows. Ethan started hacking away at vines and brush at the edge of the clearing, tossing the culled flora in a pile where he'd started a fire. Paula watched, swaying on her feet to lull Clara into a peaceful slumber.

A crack vibrated through the woods, more than just a bird on a branch. A heavier beast snapping large deadfall.

"Ethan, they're coming," she said, holding Clara close.

The family kept working, one item at a time, one foot in front of the other.

Footsteps drew closer, a frantic shuffling and stumbling across the thick forest floor. Paula's heart raced, her pulse thumping behind her eyes, filling her ears with a crescendoing hum. She looked at her family—her children, her husband—working hard, dedicated and loyal.

Her heart swelled with love and admiration.

"Paula."

Everyone stopped.

The intruder crossed the threshold, stepping over the perimeter created by Ethan and walking into the center of the clearing, hands above her head.

"Mom?" Paula said, her lip quivering.

"Honey, please," her mother said, hands still raised above her mop of silver hair. "Come home."

"Oh I will," Paula said. "Soon enough, Mom."

Her mother's eyes looked sad. Bright blue, with tears shimmering in the moonlight.

"So beautiful, you and yours," her mother said, those blue eyes looking at each member of Paula's family, drinking in their faces, settling her gaze on Clara's face. "My precious grand baby."

"Mom, you need to go now."

Her mother's face dropped, adoration replaced by stern judgement. She lowered her arms, extending them in front of her, reaching for her daughter and granddaughter. "Paula, that's enough. Give her to me. She's not what you think she is. She's only a child."

"You have no idea what we've been through, Mom. I have to think of the rest of my family. Of the ones who can be saved."

"This is lunacy, Paula! You are sick!"

Paula paused only briefly before glancing at Ethan. Ethan approached, hand on his gun.

"No," Paula said.

Ethan nodded.

He took Clara from Paula's arms and stepped away.

"Paula, no—"

Her mother didn't get more than those final two words

out before tasting the blade of Paula's knife. With one firm jab, Paula drove the blade into her mother's gaping maw and up into the roof of her mouth. Paula grabbed ahold of her mother and held the back of her head, bracing her while Ethan stepped forward and drove his palm into the handle of the knife, driving it hilt deep into the old woman's brain.

Paula kissed her mom on the cheek and let her slide to the ground. Those blue eyes stared at her the whole time.

Paula looked at Clara, sound asleep in Ethan's arms.

"We're ready," Ethan said, touching Paula's arm.

"Good," Paula said. "The rest won't be far behind."

Paula took Clara from Ethan's arms and carried her to the edge of the clearing, where Ethan had cleared off a simple, stone altar. In the distance, she could hear voices, yelling in desperation, screaming her name, screaming Clara's name.

They don't know. Paula placed her youngest on the altar. *They don't know what she is. What's inside her now.*

Hannah and Brian lit fires around the clearing, chanting and spreading herbs as the crowd drew closer to the clearing. Ethan took the shotgun and walked out into the woods, towards the mob threatening to ruin everything.

Paula acted quickly, nervous the window of opportunity would close and they would lose all hope of survival. She brought the blade down again and again, it's tip striking the stone beneath Clara's limp body. A fine mist of warm blood spurted into Paula's eyes, her mouth, and over her hands and clothes.

And Paula felt freedom.

With the dagger left embedded in her child's chest, Paula fell to her knees and watched as the blood dripped hypnotically off her golden ringlets, plip plip plipping to the earth below. And she felt a huge wave of relief, of euphoria, as Clara and the demon breathed their last breath.

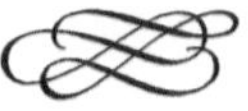

The lights were mesmerizing; turning, spinning, flashing.

The smells were intoxicating; sweet, savory, sour, earthy.

Belinda liked the way the cotton candy melted on her tongue, granular and sweet, like eating a cloud fat with crystals of rain. She stood under the strings of globe lights ranging across the entire spectrum of the rainbow, the tinny melody of the carousal grinding in the distance.

"Belle!"

Her mother beckoned her, an urgent voice through the crowd. Her mother had wanted to leave an hour ago, tired of the mass of people and the lateness of the hour. Belinda wasn't tired though. She could keep going, 'round and 'round the ferris wheel, hands coated in melted cloud, playing game after game and mounting ride after ride.

"Belle! To me, Belle! Immediately!"

Her mother meant business. Belinda knew that she was crusin' for a bruisin' if she evaded departure even one moment longer.

But the lights were so pretty, and the cotton candy so sweet.

And I'm so small, Belinda thought, ducking behind a portly man clutching a can of cheap, warm beer in his chubby hand.

Belinda ducked and dodged her way through the crowd, the smell of fried Oreos and body odour drawing her in every direction. She twisted and turned until her mother's voice was a speck in a sea of white noise, growing ever fainter as her feet padded along the dirt path.

I only need to be invisible for another moment, then she'll go the other way, try to find me by the rollercoaster. As far as the zipper, even.

Belinda wandered well past the hustle and bustle of the rides and the food and the balloons, and into the mysterious world of the tent vendors: sellers of all things eclectic and bizarre—fortune tellers, soothsayers, vagabonds peddling their wares.

Her mother's voice faded into the distance. Belinda slowed her step, taking care to stay against the tents so she could remain hidden. The crowd had thinned out this far at the edge of the carnival, and she didn't want her mother to spy her. Belinda's eyes wandered into the tents as she passed, cheap jewelry, patchwork clothing, soaps and powers and grains of every kind. The vendors were crooked and greying, a tooth here and there, scraggly white hair and long, colored braids and dreadlocks.

The tent with the talons stopped Belinda in her tracks. She lingered there, under the blue tarp, her eyes twinkling with the reflection of a hundred or more glass talons hanging from nylon cords strung up to the frame of the tent. Twinkling shade of blues and purples and blacks, shimmering and sparkling like dripping galaxies. She reached out and touched a deep purple one, stroking the smooth surface and spinning it in the light.

"You like it, dear?"

Belinda startled at the voice, a snarl doused in a wheeze. She pulled her eyes from the purple talon and looked deep into the tent at the contorted vendor. A woman, bent and shriveled, skin hanging from her frail frame in sags and stretched rolls. Nary a tooth in her head, her smile was tinged with black rot and shimmering with tacky strands of drool, her tongue thick and pressed against the roof of her smiling mouth. And her eyes, black as the talons and twinkling in the night.

"Cat got yer tongue, mah sweet?"

The woman took a step forward, leaning on a dirty ivory cane that creaked under her meager weight. Belinda stepped back, the twinkling talon spinning in her peripheral, its stars spinning, glittering...

"Uh, sorry ma'am, I's just lookin'."

"An' touchin'," the old crone said, licking her dry, cracked lips with that meaty tongue.

Belinda moved on, quick as she could, offering a nod as she left. She watched her feet, which carried her off in a sprint, and she suddenly regretted leaving the safety of her mother's voice, the comfort of her proximity. Many panting breaths later, Belinda realized she had been so intent on putting space between her and the withered vendor that she had followed the path away from the edge of the carnival and into the outlying woods.

"Mom?" she said, her voice small and sweet like the candy floss hiding in her molars. She knew full well her mother couldn't hear her, but she needed to hear the sound of a voice.

"Mama's not here."

The voice was rough, but unfamiliar. It lacked the lilt of the vendor and was punctuated by the sound of clicking teeth.

"Who..."

Belinda turned, and saw a figure, large and looming, shoulders broad and hair thick and short.

"Wandered a might out of the way, haven't we?" the man said, adjusting the brim on his shallow bowler. He wore a stained white tank top on his flabby frame, and his fingers reached for her, boney and hungry. "The carnival is the other way, my love." He slid his red-lensed glasses down to the tip of his nose and peered at her over the cracked frames. "Nothing out this far but the wolves."

Belinda should have run, but she didn't. She couldn't. In her head she screamed at her feet to go, to move, to run far, far away and find her mother and never ever come back to that horrible place. But she stood statue-still, staring into the eyes of the man with the fish-breath and elongated hands and stains on the front of his trousers...

His eyes changed. They dulled, his pupils wide and fixed, and his mouth curled into a silent scream. He stumbled backwards, revealing a third guest to the party.

The talon vendor was there, hands on her hips, clucking her tongue at the panicked man.

"She's but a girl, you whelp."

The vendor looked up to the sky, and the stars looked back at her, twinkling in the solid black between her lids.

Belinda looked away. She didn't know why—she didn't know what was going to happen—she just knew she didn't want to see it. She tucked her knees to her chest and buried her face behind her arms.

And then it happened, whatever it was. An explosion of force, of noise, of squalling and squeaking and pulsations of hot air.

Something has come. From the sky, come to take him away.

Belinda peered into the light leaking through her fingers, and saw blue and silver and purple and black raining down from the sky, twinkling with the starlight. A slice of glitter landed in front of her face. She pulled her hands away from her face to grab it.

A feather, huge and iridescent like an oil slick, dripping, warm. She slid it across her hand, and it left a trail of black crimson across her palm.

Blood.

Belinda rolled up onto her knees and wiped her hands off in the dirt. She looked up at a sky full of feathers dipped in blood and shimmering black, twirling to the ground.

It's like black, bloody rain. A featherstorm.

The vendor stood there, hunched over and wavering, one black finger extended. The finger was coated in blood, knuckle deep. The vendor gave her whole body a shake, feathers falling all around her.

"Animal," she muttered.

She clucked her tongue then dropped her chin, her eyes finding focus on Belinda's face. Her scowl turned to a grin once she locked eyes with Belinda. Belinda's blood ran cold, and she froze. The woman came to her, her movements jerky and strained. Belinda swore she could hear bones creaking beneath her layers of flesh and blood.

"You," the woman said, tapping Belinda's chest with the bloody finger. Belinda looked down. The woman turned her hand over, opening her palm. "This one, you like?"

The talon. Purple and glittery, the sharp gleam of its tip glinting in the moonlight. In that talon, Belinda could see the stars; a multitude of universes, swirling peacefully, cascading like waterfalls...

"Want?"

"Uh..." Belinda did. She really wanted it, but knew she couldn't have it. Her folks could barely afford the Value Village shoes strapped to her feet.

"Naw, chil', you want it, you do. But the question rolling about inside your head is *should* you."

Belinda nodded, a stray ringlet loosing itself from her matted bun and falling down over her freckled nose. The vendor stepped closer still, until her breath fluttered that ringlet like a pendulum over Belinda's face.

"Easy," the vendor said, closer still, their lips touching as she spoke. "You should. And you will."

Belinda grabbed it. She didn't think, didn't hesitate, just swiped it off the woman's palm, turned tail, and sprinted back through the woods, towards the lights and the sounds and the smells of the carnival. She was suddenly cold, but the talon was hot in her hand, practically searing her skin as she scrambled down the path. She held tight, though, like grasping a dying star.

In mere moments she was out in the open, sprinting past the dark tents and into the light of the carnival proper, rides and screams and tinny music singing at her from every direction. And her mother, red-faced and hands on wide hips, foot tapping a crater in the dusty ground.

"Belinda Meredith Parker," her mother said, reaching out

as Belinda screeched to a halt at her feet. "Where on earth have you been!? Wandering away in a place like this, with the likes of these," Mother waved her hand across the sea of gorked out, dirty faces, "carny folk."

"I's sorry, Momma. It's all just so pretty, and I found this—"

"No mind. Your brothers be waitin' in the car. Pray they haven't lit it aflame."

Her mother grabbed her by the scruff and dragged her through the exit without giving her so much as a once over. Belinda turned her head a few times, but was unable to make out any faces in the crowd through her mother's speed and bumpy gait. She squeezed her already clenched fist even tighter and felt the sharp tip of her treasured talon. A droplet of blood ran down her pale hand, plipping on the gravel lot as her mother tossed her into the backseat of the old station wagon.

"Eighth one in as many weeks".

The captain tapped on the photograph pinned to the board. A young woman, insides on the outside, a sequined top laying nearby in a puddle of mud. Belinda recognized the location. It was just down the street from the park she used to play at as a child.

"No connection, no similarities."

Next photo, a young black man splayed out inside a dumpster, neck twisted so he had a good view of his own ass.

The captain's finger slid to the next photograph on the board.

A child.

Nobody looked.

"So what do we have, other than nothing?"

"The red toque," a young blue offered from the back of the conference room.

"Yes," the captain said, chewing his lower lip. "The toque."

Belinda checked out. She could hear the voices in her head, a muffled rehashing of tired old information. The precinct had been talking about the red toque killer for weeks —hell, the whole city was focused on nothing but. Victims were piling up, each death more violent than the last, with nary a lead other than a perp in a red toque caught on camera loitering around several of the crime scenes. Other than that, lots of blood, lots of death, and little else.

Belinda fiddled with the cuffs on her belt, chewed-to-the-quick nails scraping against the steel, when a firm grip clasped her shoulder.

"Jesus fucking Christ, Barry."

"I can't believe we gotta deal with this shit," he said.

"What'd we draw?"

"Northeast."

Fuck.

The murders were spread across all quadrants of the city, but the Northeast was the worst for many reasons. Nothing to suggest another murder might occur there, but there were enough illicit substances and non-consensual fellatio to make things uncomfortable and torturous for a beat cop.

"Problem?" Barry asked, a smile twerking the corner of his mouth.

Smug prick.

It had been a lifetime of misogyny, both subtle and potent as a punch in the face. Belinda had flown from the nest at the ripe old age of sixteen, shacking up with a teacher who promised her escape from her childhood for the small price of loyalty and on-demand blowjobs. After a few years of that mess, Belinda created an escape of her own, using syringes and deals that brought enough green to furnish a living space of her own.

That's about as much power as she could muster.

She gave up the life, trading needles for a mop, and sustained her life by cleaning houses and office buildings. That led her to a cleaning contract with the local police department. There, she went from mop to mailroom, mailroom to reception, and a training program with the actual blues.

Even now, donning a uniform and her very own weapon, she was still that young woman with a needle in her arm, squirming beneath the thumbs of the men in charge.

"There's no problem, Barry," she said, feigning a casual smile. "Except the serial killer, that is."

"Ah, we won't get a piece o' that," Barry said, his hands on her shoulders, finger crawling lower over her collarbone. She shrugged him off and stood.

"How's that?" she asked, ignoring the daily advance.

"Nothing but sticky hookers and rusty needles up that way. Nothing for a pretty little thing like you to be scared of."

But she was scared. Always. At every turn, every darkness, every noise and movement and sound. She had spent her life scrambling, running, powerless, and even now, with a weapon on her hip and a badge on her pocket, she was a pawn and a plaything. A joke.

"Except the serial killer," she reiterated.

"Except him, yeah. I suppose." Barry moved in closer. She tried to not step back, tried to stand her ground, but she couldn't. Her boot moved back an inch. He noticed. He smiled. "I'll protect you, sweetheart."

He reached out and stroked her cheek, then turned and walked past the horde of blues loitering around the coffeepot. They looked at her and chuckled. She gulped a breath, trying to stay the tears welling in her eyes. Her fingers crawled up her chest to the top button of her uniform and beneath, touching the glittering midnight talon hanging from the cord around her neck.

Her heart slowed and her anxiety quieted.

It always did when she touched that talon filled with stars and horrible beauty.

There's a certain magic in its terror, she thought. It brought her mind to a place where there was nothing but her and the woods, mangled tree branches reaching for her, protecting her. And a beautiful cascade of raining feathers, black and shimmering, fluttering down from the moonlit sky...

"Dreaming of dresses and boyfriends again?" the captain said as he passed, giving her a firm cuff on the shoulder. "Get on it, Belle."

Fuck you, she thought, and the feathers in her mind fluttered a little quicker.

"Yes sir," she said, averting her eyes to the floor.

She grabbed the keys to the cruiser off the hook, and Barry immediately snatched them out of her hand.

"I drive," he said, walking out of the station.

He always drives.

THE NORTHEAST WAS sticky and dark, a sludge of smoke and sex hanging thick in the air. The inside of the cruiser was worse, the smell of Barry's sweat and half-eaten donair lingering in the tight space. Belinda opened her window, turning her face to the air to prevent claustrophobia from clamping on her lungs like a vice. They rolled up and down the streets, consuming the visual buffet of scantily clad women, young bucks prowling the streets in dark hoodies, channeling their inner Corey Hart by donning the darkest of sunglasses on the dimmest of nights. On a bus bench, an old man—as long in the tooth as the beard down his chest—lay bleeding from his nose, eyes fixed on a distant nowhere.

"Should we check him?" Belinda asked.

"Naw," Barry said, not even looking. "Darwin will take care of that one."

They rolled on, passing dark alleys ripe with mournful cries of pain and pleasure, the last shred of humanity nowhere to be found.

Barry pulled the cruiser into the handicapped spot in front of a battered convenience story.

"Grabbing fags," he said, motioning to the empty cigarette box on the dash. "Want anything?"

"No, I'm fine, thanks."

Barry got out of the car and Belinda breathed a sigh of relief. She relished any stolen minute she could let her guard down. She gazed through the yellowed glass of the convenience store at the twitching fluorescent lights and customers hovering silently in line, their eyes glued on smart phones, arms full of chips and jerky and cheap, horse-piss beer. She looked up and down the street and the cold, wet pavement, piles of trash here and there, unsavory population skulking in the shadows.

I need a shower, she thought, as she tugged at the collar of her uniform. Her finger brushed along the talon. She was surprised at how warm it was. She pinched it between her fingers, wondering if the heat was increasing on her fingertips or in her imagination. Sweat beaded on her upper lip, and she felt her breath and heart quicken.

I have to get out.

She wrenched open the door and jumped from the car, her abrupt exit drawing the attention of a couple of corner crawlers. She brushed her hands down her uniform, trying to be nonchalant, and shut the door with less vigor than she had opened it.

The night air was not fresh, but it was better than being stuck in that car. She meandered back and forth in front of the store, glancing at the posters and graffiti plastered over the brick of the building and the rusted paint of the light poles and mailbox. The song of the city played out to her, the beeping of horns and coughs of addicts.

And weeping.

Is that someone crying?

Belinda looked behind, searching for the lungs behind the mewl, but saw only grey and weathered men, and a cock-sure pro strutting on 4 inch spikes.

Squeee...

The sound was trickling out from the mouth of a nearby alley. No one around seemed too concerned, but the sound was horrible and pleading, like a tortured animal. Belinda looked into the convenience store. Barry was chatting up a tall drink of water in a translucent white dress with ruby lipstick smudged across her yellowed-teeth. Belinda shook her head.

He'll be another good while.

The first few steps towards the alley were simple, just another few meters of the pacing she had already begun. The last meter before her eyes could turn the corner were nearly impossible to traverse, her feet growing heavier with each step, the light growing impossibly dimmer.

She didn't think. She couldn't, or her feet would refuse to proceed. She rounded the corner and entered the mouth of the alley, its black, gaping maw swallowing her whole. Her right hand wrapped around the metal shaft of her torch and her left grasped the talon around her neck.

Hot, she thought.

She walked along the brick wall, stepping gingerly over trash bags and puddles of vomit and urine, trying not to upset anything that might make a racket. After she was deeply inserted into the alley, she stopped and put her back against the wall to survey her surroundings.

Her eyes had adjusted to the dark. The streetlights didn't lick the alley, their hazy light ending at the lone entrance. The alley was narrow, enough room for a single vehicle—a van or garbage truck, if need be—but not much else. She doubted any vehicles passed this way, though, considering the amount of rubbish and debris littering the pocked and potholed lane. The surrounding buildings towered over her, four story brick apartment buildings, fire-ladders descending from warped and dated walkways.

The alley was still. Belinda let her eyes settle on the pavement, her vision flitting to follow the occasional rat or blowing piece of rubbish. The noise from the street behind her dampened, leaving only the rustling of the mundane in front of her.

She took a step forward, then another step, the light from her torch manic, moving from surface to surface, texture to structure, finding nothing but the inconsequential. A stained mattress leaning against a wall, piles of trash bags leaking foods and fluids and maggots, an overturned shopping cart.

And deeper still, until the noise behind her sounded a million miles away, and her light was but a gleam down a tunnel, black and empty.

And the mewl.

The cry.

Screeee…

Her torch light found the young man, curled in a ball, sliced and slashed and quavering in the filth of the alley. He was naked, save a single sock, which was missing the toe, revealing the absence of toes that should have been beneath the wool. She shone the light on his face, and his bladder released, along with a wail from the pit of his belly.

"It's okay," she said, her voice soft and unsure. She held out her hand, not really sure what she was offering.

"I'm a police officer."

Barely, the voice in her head scoffed.

"You're safe now."

Not even a bit, the voice taunted.

The young man shook his head, his body erupting into spastic terror as she approached. She stopped and looked into his eyes, icy blue, filled with fear and pain and torture.

And not looking at her.

Looking *over* her.

Vomit bubbled in her throat, a burning that made her eyes water. She turned.

"Hello, bitch."

Belinda couldn't return the greeting. Her heart wrapped her voice in talons of its own, its violent beating threatening to split her ribs.

A red toque, was all she thought, looking up at the man's head. *We were right.*

He hovered between her and the escape route from the alley, his massive frame rocking back and forth, casting dancing shadows in the cloak of darkness. A line of spittle twirled from his fat lower lip. He licked it off with a thick, meaty tongue, his breath potent even from a meter away.

Belinda screamed. Not because of his bloodstained shirt or the Bowie knife in his hand. Not because of the jagged teeth that she recognized from the bite marks in victims two and four. But because of the searing pain on her chest, and the smell of burning flesh.

The talon had gone from warm to hot to blue-fire in a matter of seconds, shooting pain through her every nerve ending. She clawed at her chest and ripped the talon off her neck. It stuck to her hand, melting into her flesh with white-hot intensity. She dropped to her knees, screaming bloody murder as the actual murderer stood at arm's length. She tried to pull the talon off, but it had melted right into her flesh.

Then, in an instant, the pain was gone. She looked at her hand, turning it over a few times, back and forth. Her skin was unscathed, but her middle finger was black, glittering and gleaming even in the dark of the alley, the tip as sharp as the point of a blade.

Red Toque coughed. Belinda lifted her head. His head was cocked, curious but ever the opportunist, she imagined. He was over top of her, his blade hoisted in the air, his lifted arm exposing the flab of his hairy gut.

It didn't require consideration or deliberate action.

It simply happened, out of her control.

She swiped.

Her hand came out, and her middle finger slashed across his abdomen, squelching knuckle-deep through flesh and muscle and organ.

Belinda scrambled back on her haunches, expecting a dam of blood to release, or even the escape of an organ or two. But none of that happened. The perp stood erect, stunned and still, until the pain set in. He grabbed at his gut and fell to the ground, clutching his newly acquired gash and squealing like a stuck pig.

There was no blood. No guts, no fluids, no organs.

There was burning flesh, though. The mark from the talon started smoking, black edges glowing red, eating the wound and charring the flesh around it millimeter by millimeter. It kept going as the man patted his skin, trying to put out a fire that wasn't there.

He peeled like an onion. Flesh and muscle and tendon peeled back, all the blood and fluids contained within his sheath evaporating into steam.

Belinda looked away. She could still smell what was going on, still hear it, but she didn't want to see. She couldn't. With her hands over her eyes, she began to hum Faelith's lullaby, rocking back and forth on her haunches.

Is it coming for him? That thing from above?

Curiosity had plagued her through all her years, from the very moment the first featherstorm had hit. Oh how she wished she would have looked, would have seen her savior from above, come to carry her fear away on those beautiful wings...

She sat up, hands still over her face, and opened her eyes, forcing herself to peek through the slats of her fingers.

Disbelief drew her to her feet. The murderer was on the ground. He had peeled off all his clothes, save his stained, white briefs. His body was bloated and blistered, black ooze seeping out of the talon gash across his gut. Like a virus, a conglomeration of black worming masses was spreading from his gash, crawling and gyrating beneath his bright white skin until his whole body was marred by squiggling black veins.

They moved, and with every twist and curve and pulsation, he bellowed in agony.

Then he burst.

Like a million tiny talons, feathers sprouted through his pores, sloughing the skin off his body and slicing the muscle and tendon from his bones. His head remained, but his body was a quivering mass of feathers, wet with residual blood and gore and dense globs of fat.

Red Toque heaved and rocked himself to his feet, his bones cracking and creaking until he was erect. He stood a good two feet taller than he had before. A cage of black, shiny bone had locked around his skeleton, like hundreds of tiny hands clasping and clawing to hold his bones in place.

And the head. Not his head, but the other head. An enormous naked skull with a bat snout and bulbous cranium had affixed itself to the man's spine. A black, leathery tongue slipped between its sharp, cracked canines, grazing Red Toque's cheek and slicing it like a fine razor blade.

"Please!" he pleaded to her, to no one, to everyone. "Make it stop! Make it let go!"

Belinda knew. Like a switch had clicked in her brain, she looked down at her middle finger. Only it wasn't her original finger. Her new finger was rock hard, midnight purple, and sharp as the edge of a blade.

She looked up at the sky.

My savior's not coming from the stars.

Not coming.

Going.

She leaned in to the writhing perp with the leathery lizard-rodent growing out of his spine and whispered in both their ears.

"Fly."

The perp's body went rigid and his arms shot out to the side. Leathery wings with long black feathers unfolded, spanning the entire width of the alley. A scream emanated from his throat as the creature attached to him manipulated his body like a marionette. The rodential-reptilian driver looked into Belinda's eyes, and its mouth curled into a bloody, wide smile. She gave it a single nod. It took a deep breath and pushed off, its grand wings pushing her down with a powerful blast of air as it shot to the sky. The wings pumped and flapped, and with every hoist and heave, Red Toque screamed. He screamed in agony, in delirium, in absolute horror at the realization that he was being carried away to his fate.

Belinda cried.

It was beautiful.

So beautiful.

It its wake, the creature left a tornado of feathers raining down upon the alley, blotting out the stars with a glitter and twinkle of their own. Belinda stood, turned her face to the sky, and twirled through the feathers, a macabre ballet, smiling as blood-touched clumps of purple and black stuck to her tear drenched face.

"What in the actual fuck is this?"

Barry's voice was an abrasive interruption in the beauty that surrounded her. Feathers continued raining down from above, and Belinda kept twirling in the downpour.

A featherstorm.

Belinda looked down at her hand and wiggled her fingers, admiring her new talon.

She turned and looked at Barry, at the exposed flesh on his forearm, his throat.

I only need access to a small bit...

His eyes widened as he looked into her eyes, solid black and sparkling with stars.

And she smiled.

DEATH YOU SERVED

The rickety bus creaked and heaved, fumes vomiting from its tailpipe as it trembled down the old road. Mia and Sachia held on to each other, watching as the barren wasteland outside raced by the windows.

"We'll be there promptly, girls."

The driver's voice was wet and wrapped in a cackle that couldn't quite find an escape.

Mia shuddered. Tears glazed her eyes.

"It's okay," Sachia said, squeezing Mia's hand. "We'll be there soon."

She doesn't mean it, Mia thought. *She's still angry.*

As if on cue, the home appeared over the lip of the next hill, staring in wait up the road at its feet.

"Will it hurt?" Mia asked the older girl.

"No," Sachia said.

"Will it be frightening?"

Sachia didn't answer.

Mia looked out the window. The bus had slowed considerably, throwing up a minimal cloud of dust. Tumbleweeds blew across the ground, catching in cracks and bouncing into the air.

"Will I, too, blow away to dust?" Mia asked.

Sachia said nothing.

Mia wasn't ready. When the bus pulled up to the behemoth of a structure, she remained firmly planted to her seat, even after Sachia stood.

"C'mon," Sachia whispered, a hint of panic escaping its constraints. "Don't linger. They'll come out and get you, regardless."

Mia got to her feet, despite the lead in her stomach. She shuffled down the aisle, Sachia tugging her sleeve the whole way.

The air should have been fresh, should have helped to quash Mia's fear, but it didn't. It wasn't fresh. It wasn't anything. It was a stale, stagnant yellow blanket that hovered in Mia's nostrils and lungs; tight and still and bland. A suffocating nothingness.

"It's not warm," Mia said, her voice breaking. "It's not cold. It's not anything."

"Hush," Sachia said, jabbing her sister in the ribs.

The headmistress stood on the step, patiently awaiting their arrival. She was stunning, Mia noticed straight away, with a black dress and blue-black hair. She was beautiful and terrifying, pale skin glowing from beneath the slits and ties of the dark fabric.

"Promptly now, girls," the driver said, rushing the stragglers off the bus. "We haven't much time before I fetch the next lot of you."

And with that, the last of the girls, two young beauties that looked almost old enough to drink, were off the bus and waiting in a trembling cluster at the base of the front steps. The bus pulled away, clouds of silence billowing in its wake.

There was no wind, no animals, no one was talking. The headmistress stared into each and every set of eyes. No one dared allow breath to pass their lips. A buzzard cawed in the distance, the sound of nails down a chalkboard. Mia startled, and Sachia held her tighter. The headmistress met Mia's eyes, and for the briefest of moments, Mia thought she saw a smile threaten to emerge across the woman's stoic face.

A gasp rippled through the pack of girls when the headmistress spun around, her raven-coloured hair whirling in a pirouette as she clip-clopped into the house. The girls looked at each other, eyes pleading for a prompt, for a suggestion, for a hero that would lead the way.

One girl, a strawberry blond with a burgundy bow in her hair, took the first step. Her bravery opened the dam, and the girls moved in unison, up the stairs and into the house like a swarm.

The inside of the house smelled of campfires and copper,

and the air was wet and heavy. Though beautiful on the outside, its interior was dilapidated, yellowed walls peeling strips of paint and ceilings sagging and stained brown.

"What is that smell?" Mia asked, tugging on Sachia's sleeve.

"Shhh," Sachia scolded, swatting her sister's hand.

"But it smells so awful," Mia said, tears welling again. "Like the slaughterhouse—"

"Because it is," Sachia snapped, raising her finger to her lips in an attempt at silencing her frantic sibling.

They moved from the entrance into the main room, which happened to be the only room on the first floor. A massive wood stove sat against the far wall, covered in pots roiling with steam. Long wooden benches lined the room like church pews, empty, save scraps of food and chipped dishes.

The strawberry blonde hesitated only a moment before walking forward and taking a seat at the end of a pew in the first row, folding her hands neatly in her lap like the proper miss she clearly was. The others followed suit, but with much less grace, stumbling and seating themselves with an awkward hesitance.

"What are we doing?" Mia asked, looking around the room. It was barren, except for the wood stove, pews, and meager leavings of occupants passed. "What is this?"

Sachia didn't answer.

She's done answering, Mia thought. *She's angry.*

Mia looked around at the other faces, pale and sullen,

streaks of dusty tears marring blotchy skin. A small girl, no more than five, was trembling violently, despite the tepid air.

So young. How is she here?

The little girl looked up at her with wide blue eyes, lip trembling, blonde hair soaked in brown crud.

So young.

They ate in silence. Bowls of gruel from a pot on the wood stove were doled out by a hefty woman in a burlap dress, mouth stitched closed, nostrils flaring to accommodate the influx of air. Mia cringed when the woman handed her the bowl. The woman paused, smiling, the heavy twine stitching her lips together tearing her flesh ever so slightly.

That twine is damp with blood, Mia thought, her eyes fixed on the meaty, cracked lips. *That'll infect in no time.*

The smiling henchwoman waddled away, gristle dripping from her ladle to the floor. Mia did not eat. She held the bowl in her hand, watching globs of meat float around the brown sludge.

"It's time." A bald woman with thick veins protruding from her head stood in the doorway, filling it with her great mass of muscle. "Five at a time. No dawdling."

"At least it'll be quick," Sachia said.

Mia eyed the girls lining the pews. Twenty. At most.

Too quick, Mia thought, her heart pummeling her ribcage.

The strawberry blonde, who had proudly taken the first spot in the first row of pews, now looked like she deeply regretted that decision. She was in the first five. She wasn't so quick to lead this time.

"Let's go," the bald woman barked.

The strawberry blonde looked at the girls, her eyes frantic and too afraid to cry. Everyone looked away as if ashamed by her weakness. Her sobs became audible, and her body convulsed with tremors of fear. The bald woman rolled her eyes and stepped forward. She wore heavy, shiny black boots that crept up to her exposed groin, the laces threaded straight through the muscular flesh on her thighs. Those heavy boots clopped so loud Mia was sure they would break right through the floor. The bald, booted woman grabbed a handful of strawberry blonde hair, and lifted the girl off the pew. The girl screamed and writhed, but the bald woman didn't flinch. She held the girl, suspended a good foot off the floor, and walked out of the room.

The next four girls followed without argument, looking at their feet rather than their violently struggling comrade. Mia watched as they exited the room, feet shuffling, eyes darting around. It pained her to see their fear, their uncertainty. She looked back down at her gruel.

Time passed. Maybe minutes, an hour, Mia couldn't be sure. The room was quiet, except for the growling of tummies, and the occasional whimper from someone who couldn't hold their fear any longer. Just when Mia thought the tension might turn her inside out, a crash came from the upper floor. A girl in the pew ahead of her screamed.

"What was that?" Mia asked, searching Sachia's face.

Sachia didn't answer. She was looking up at the ceiling, watching the candle-lit chandelier swaying from the boom.

Another boom. And another.

Five in all.

Then silence again, other than the tinkling of the yellowed crystals on the swaying chandelier. The girls looked up, watching the light dancing off the walls as it swayed to a stop.

"C'mon then," a voice boomed. "On with it."

The bald woman was once again standing in the doorway. Her platform boots were still laced to her long legs, but Mia had not heard her clomping down the stairs. When she left the room, though, she was clomping, even louder than before. The second batch of girls didn't waste any time, following close behind the sound of the boots.

Mia wished she was with them.

The wait was agonizing.

The crashes were louder this time. The floor above creaked, and gyprock rained down in a fine powder with each of the five booms. But this time, there were screams. Blood-curdling and high-pitched, gargling and desperate. Mia looked up at the ceiling, and saw the water spots along the trim growing darker, wetter...

The next batch of girls were already standing at the door before the woman appeared from the foyer. These girls did not go quietly. The bangs were accompanied by ear-piercing mewling and gagging sobs. The walls shook, the wood cracking from ceiling to floor with bang after bang after bang.

Mia's pew was the last one left. By the time the bald woman was standing in the doorway, Mia was regretting wishing the time away. She did not want to go. She did not wish for it to be all over. That room, with those splintered pews and that nauseating gruel and that terrible, horrible woman with the stitched smile didn't seem all that bad now. Mia could comfortably see herself spending an eternity there, bottom full of sores from being pressed onto that wood, stomach burning from consumption of that lardy stew.

Now, staring at the back of those boots, at the platform heels and blood spurting from the holes in the bald woman's thighs, Mia thought the room with the pews had been paradise.

Up the stairs they went, avoiding holes and missing boards. Mia stumbled and reached for the handrail, but quickly recoiled when she grasped something slick and wet.

Not a handrail.

A taught set of braided intestines, perhaps from three or four donors, attached at the top and bottom of the stairs on large femur bones.

"Keep going," Sachia said, pulling her sister up the stairs.

The top of the stairs had a tiny entryway that opened up into one large room that occupied the entire top floor of the house. The ceiling was high, like a gymnasium, and the walls were soiled and weathered, very much like the room below.

This room was more barren than that room, though. Virtually empty…

Except for the bodies strewn across the floor.

Mia followed her sister into the room, and her feet sank into the shag carpet. Her toes squished like she was stepping in mud at the bog back home. She wiggled them, grinding into the moisture.

"Girls."

The bald woman was gone. The raven-haired headmistress had taken her place, standing in the center of the room.

Had she been there when we came in? Mia wondered.

"Noses against the wall, girls."

Nobody moved. Mia looked at the other girls, eyebrows raised, eyes scouring the walls.

The headmistress drew in a deep breath that sucked the air out of the room. All the girls looked at her. Her eyes turned red, and her mouth flew open, splitting her head in two. A tail sprouted between her legs, and teeth jutted from the bottom of her jaw.

"I said, noses against the fucking wall, ladies!"

It wasn't a voice. It was a feral howl, a morbid bellow that clawed its way into Mia's ears and dove to the bottom of her colon.

The girls obeyed. Instantly.

It was a pleasant surprise, that wall. It smelled of lavender and honey.

"Sachia?" Mia said, reaching to the side for her sister. "It smells like Mom. Like home. Isn't it lovely, Sachia?"

Sachia didn't answer. Mia turned to look at her. Sachia's face was pressed against the wall, a smile on her plump lips. Mia's heart was swollen with love for her beautiful sister, her mentor, her caregiver. Her best friend.

Mia yelped as her cheek split open. A tongue, thin and black and barbed, licked across her cheek and in front of her face.

"Against the wall," the headmistress hissed. "Dear."

Mia focused on the wall but watched Sachia in her peripheral. *Odd. She seems taller, higher...*

The lavender and honey was overwhelming. Mia's nose pressed into the wall, and it received her, soft and supple like her mother's breast. Mia felt euphoric, like walking on air, and the pleasure intensified. She breathed in and tasted her favourite cookies that Mother used to bake—chocolate chip with caramel drizzle. Mia licked the wall, and her tongue was overwhelmed with the flavours of a hundred favourite meals.

Then came unfamiliar sensations. The smell of lilies on a wedding day that had yet to transpire, the pulsation and flood of sexuality yet to be released, the pure adoration of birth and child rearing.

Pleasure turned to desperation, and then to abject terror.

Mia had never felt those lovely things.

She never would.

She opened her eyes and turned her head away from the wall.

"Sachia," she whispered.

Sachia didn't answer. She couldn't. She would never answer again. Her face was contorted in pain and horror and violation, the front of her white nightgown soaked in crimson. Mia looked down at the waterfall of blood pouring to the carpet and found that she and her sister—all the girls—were suspended several feet off the floor.

Mia looked down at her body. She, too, was but a painting hung on the wall, suspended by a talon that reached into her from beyond the chipped paint, from the opposite side of the house and the hell that lay beyond.

"Hurt?" The raven woman hissed.

Yes! Mia screamed, but only in her head. Her words were muted by the blood pouring from her mouth.

"Good," the raven woman said.

Mia felt it, in that talon that ripped through her skin and grasped her organs. She felt the receiving end of the blade she had driven into her own mother. She felt Sachia's hands as they had wrapped around her neck after discovering their mother's body in the master bed.

She turned to her sister, hanging on that wall, face blue and petechial hemorrhaging brightening her eyes to a glowing red, tears bleeding down her face.

She feels her own hands, like they wrapped around my throat, when she saw what I had done...

"Feel the death you served," the raven-haired woman said from her perch on the wall.

Mia fell.

She fell for many minutes, crashing to that wet carpet, sending blood splashing up and coating the walls, filling her mouth and eyes and ears...

She saw herself fall.

Her body was limp on the ground, a pile of meat flayed out and on display, just like she had left her dear mother.

She looked to the side, at all the other girls, covered in blood, embedded in and beneath the walls, floating, lining the house in horizontal stacks and piles that extended out into the barren wasteland beyond the structure itself. The rows of girls floated for miles.

And in the distance, a plume of dust from the bus approached on the horizon.

TO NEVER KNOW

Eyes, blue and brown, grey and hazel, floating in jars, fixed in vacant wonder. Light poured from the industrial bulbs above, coating the eyes in glistening tears. But the eyes were not sad. They were nothing, just orbs of fibrous tissue, empty and unfeeling. In them, I imagined a haunted joy, an innocence unaware of the harsh reality of their demise. Next to the eyes were jars of bones. Tiny, delicate bones.

"What are you thinking?" the CSI asked.

"I'm thinking that some days—most days—I hate the world."

I poked a gloved finger at a jar as if to challenge its reality. It really was there. Unfortunately. The room was as barren as the eyes, devoid of warmth, decency, and beauty. An operating table, top of the line medical equipment, and lights.

Horrible lights, benign on their own, but menacing in relation to the product of their illumination. They shone down on the single jar whose cold glass still lingered on the pad of my finger, and on the jars lining the cupboards. Forty-eight, in fact, each containing a pair of eyes.

On the counter below the jars of eyes were several trays. I walked over and put my nose down to one of the trays. *They are like little shells. Souvenirs from a day at the beach or some exotic location.* But they were not shells, and their origin was not tropical nor exotic. They were bones. Tiny bones, many bones, some still stained with the signature of their owner's blood. Bones so small, so wispy and delicate they could have come from the bodies of baby birds. But I knew.

Then there was the bassinet. A clean cradle containing a little blanket adorned with pastel ducks, swaddled around the fragile patient, cloud-white bandages taped over her eyes and ears. Medical staff conducted their triage with calm intensity, the tiny angel's vitals showing stable on the plethora of monitors hovering above her nest.

"Detective," a voice beckoned from outside.

I didn't need much coaxing to retreat out those cellar doors. As bright as it had been under the flood lights, the mid-morning sun still blinded me. It was a beautiful day outside, but dark and stormy behind my eyes. I did not raise a hand to block the sun. I wanted the warmth to breach my surface and flood my bloodstream. If that didn't work, I hoped the searing rays would burn straight through my retinas and erase all the horror I had seen.

"Psych's on the way to take her downtown for assessment. You want a crack at her first?" asked a beat cop, some lackey first responder.

"Don't need to," I said. "We have enough evidence to string 'er up. Besides, I go at her before psych does, it'd be inadmissible anyways."

"Yeah, but aren't you the least bit curious?"

I was. Morbidly so. I hated myself for it, but I yearned to crawl inside her mind and find out what preceded this particular brand of lunacy.

I was a good jaunt from the front door of the demon's lair. I took long strides, hoping to minimize the time the journey would consume and therefore my time at that horror show, but my surroundings contradicted my hustling fear. Children, playing and laughing, oblivious to the flurry of law enforcement buzzing around like locusts. Beautiful young hearts, dancing, singing. I couldn't bear to watch them lest my stomach claw its way up into my throat. The birds sang in rhythm with my footfalls, peaceful and melodic, attempting to carry my heavy feet on the wings of their song. *Damn this place, this illusion of the devil.* Evil wears this utopia of contentment and peace like a mask.

She was cuffed and seated on a floral chesterfield, sipping tentatively on a tea of sweet chamomile or peppermint or some other delicate flavour that had no business passing her lips. I wanted to swat it out of her hands and penetrate her ivory flesh with the shards. Instead, I took my place across from her.

"Ma'am," I said, clenching my fists.

"You don't think that," she said, looking at me over her long lashes, eyes swollen from crying.

"Think what?"

"That I deserve a moniker as respectful as *ma'am*. To you, I am not human. I am just another deviant; you believe me to be a vicious perpetrator. You don't understand."

"I don't, no. Will you explain?"

"Why? Will it change your mind?"

"Change my mind? In regard to what? Your guilt? Your sickness? Not likely."

"The world's sickness. The solution."

"They were children. *Babies*."

"And they still are," she said, looking out the window and gushing with a mother's pride. "They are, and they will grow. They will become beautiful, autonomous adults in an otherwise depraved world of lemmings. No one has died here, Detective. Consider that."

I looked out at the frolicking youth who were playing without a care, without knowledge of their torment, their mutilation.

"Do you tire of it, Detective?"

"Tire of what? People like you?"

"The senseless violence. The hate. I can't sit by and

condone it any longer. No one should. Day after day, death after death, hate upon hate, force fed to us until our minds are bloated and splitting at the seams, so completely satiated with negativity that we vomit." She took a sip of her tea, her slender hands shaking with rage. "We purge the overindulged meals of our sensory inundation, the excess manifesting itself in the form of more hate, more violence. The cycle is eternal."

I couldn't look at her. More accurately, I couldn't look away from the children. Chasing each other, stumbling, laughing. So innocent. So oblivious.

"There is a darkness in all of us, sure," she continued. "But it's how that darkness grows, how it is *fed* that is destroying us as a species."

The children ran through the flowers, rolled in the dew-kissed petals, inhaling deeply the aromatic sweetness, and sneezing with laughter in their bellies.

"Once upon a time, after I first received my medical degree, I wondered what it would be like to never know," she mused. "To never know the lies and hate we are force-fed by the media, by our families, by our neighbours. To never know the anger and hate that unites the lost and lonely in the worst way possible."

Balls bounced, rolling from tiny, fumbling palms.

"Every day we are assaulted with campaigns *against* rather than *for*. We need to be unified by more than our disdain, but it's easier to be angry, especially when others are.

Hate is a vivid emotion and intoxicating when one craves exhilaration."

Laughter. Hugs. Smiles. Ringlets bouncing in the gentle breeze.

"The children? They don't know. They'll never know, not to the toxic levels that we do. The sludge of the world has been forced into us through our fingertips by social media, and through the voices of biased media. But these children will never see it, never hear it. They will only hear the beating of their own hearts, and see the world through their mind's eyes, eyes that haven't been burdened by ignorant hysteria and groupthink. And they are better for it, to live like this. To never know."

I saw a little boy outside. He was five, maybe six. He was strong and healthy, a tad on the stocky side, skin rosy from fresh air and glee. His eyes could have been beautiful, but I would never know for sure. No one would. They were one of many sets of eyes contained in that cellar, removed at birth, along with the hammer, anvil, and stirrup bones from his ears. Conducted as a standard procedure akin to the removal of a foreskin would be, the eyes and the ear bones were excised from the children, all forty-eight of them, shortly after birth. This woman had thrown a wrench in the social devolution of our species. At first blush it seemed barbaric, but...

"They were all fed at their mothers' breasts, all cuddled at night when they cried and burped when they were gassy," she said, sounding like a proud grandparent. "The parents are here, on the compound. They agreed to everything. And the children are better for it."

Outside the children were running around, playing with each other and interacting with the world in a way that was foreign to me, to most of society. Relying only on the senses that remained, they knew nothing of race, of judgement, of intolerance. They recognized the smell of the trees, the kind touch of familiar hands, the taste of food to nourish and satisfy them.

Her voice was light and airy. Proud. "The older ones, they read, Detective. Braille. We have teachers on site. And they ride bikes, have pets, cook and clean and sew..."

They knew fear only as a result of danger or experiences of displeasure, but not because of assumption. And hate had not soiled the mental construction of their world. Their lives were about functionality and primal relations. Beautiful and savage.

"To never know is better, don't you think?" she asked.

In this world? It's better not to think.

"Bring thine coffee, wench!"

Gem shouted in the direction of the kitchen, his commanding voice booming off the stone walls of the tavern. There was no rustling and bustling, no clinking and clanking of cutlery or mug. Nothing but his belly's gurgling desire for the bean.

"I heareth no breweth!" Gem bellowed again. He hammered the table with a large fist, punctuating his demand.

He was answered by a disrespectful silence, a taunting beyond the swinging doors leading to the kitchen.

Gem sighed and heaved forward, rocking out of his chair. He was irritated to have to leave his throne and the warmth of his fire, but more concerned about the help, who rarely ignored his demands. But mostly, he needed his black gold. He clopped across the wooden floor, his bootfalls echoing through his bones, until he reached the entrance to the kitchen.

He stopped.

A heaviness engulfed his chest and belly. He grimaced as the phantom lifting stone perched itself upon his lungs, a heavy burden shared by the ache in his left arm.

Gem swung open the rickety doors, which announced his arrival with a troll's groan. Once in the kitchen, he let the doors swing shut, and they retaliated, smacking him on his ass. He grunted, but his eyes remained focused on their target.

"Ah shit," Gem sighed, running clubbed fingers through his mane of white hair. "Yer here, eh, you sick bitch."

The creature in the kitchen nodded, the bones in its neck creaking and crackling with the slightest tilt of its head.

"Well," Gem said, puffing his chest. "Let's get to it, then."

The creature floated forward, ethereal black robes encircling her like toxic mist, limbs neon white against the rustic copper of the old kitchen.

"Wait," Gem said, holding up his hand.

The creature paused, misty tendrils sling-shotting ahead of it. Gem grimaced as the black smoke-robe came within a faerie's hair of his cheek.

"Right now?" Gem asked. "This instant? Here?"

The creature nodded, its hood rippling around the empty expanse of a face hole.

"Need I cease here, in the help's working quarters?" Gem said. "In a place of meat juices, vegetable trimmings, and soiled silverware?"

The creature shrugged, white bony palms facing the heavens.

"C'mon, ye ol' bitch," Gem growled. "Lemme walk my land once more. A brief stroll to the cliff to overlook my kingdom. Allow my eyes to close on the sight of my conquests."

Hesitation fluttered the creature's movements. Gem held his breath but also his ground, feigning courage in the face of his worst fear.

Gem stared.

The creature stilled.

Gem jumped when the creature swept its hand towards the exit.

A gesture of concession.

"Atta bitch," Gem said, reaching out to pat the creature's back.

He quickly came to his senses and retracted his hand.

"Well then. We be off, now."

Gem spun on his heels and swung through the kitchen doors again. One last time. He headed to the massive oak door of his home and tavern.

And, one last time, strutted out of his musty abode into the green utopia of his world.

He dropped to his knees, panic contributing kilograms to the stone upon his chest.

The creature reached for his hand.

"No!" he bellowed, the words a cannon from his seizing throat. "Another moment. Please."

The creature retreated, folding elongated arms across an empty chest.

Gem struggled, his breath battling pressure in the pit of his stomach. He drove his fists into the rich soil, squelching between his fingers as he tried to stand.

He could not.

The stone was too heavy, and the cobra too tight.

He raised his eyes to signal defeat, but movement drew his gaze away from the dark creature.

To his left, amidst the vines and sprigs of growth, were his men; his brothers in arms, heads held high, hearts glowing with the love of brotherhood. A knight walked forward, boots lightly skimming the ground until his hand lay upon Gem's chest.

"Brother," he said. "We stand united. Always."

The knight stood and retreated, his boots leaving deep imprints in the muck, his legs straining as if traversing thick, wet cement.

Gem stood, the weight of the stone on his chest significantly lessened.

He looked at the dark creature.

"I be fine, you wretch," he spat. "Don't go gettin' your knickers in a knot jus' yet. I ain't done doin'."

Gem trudged forward, the creature riding his shadow. After ten meters, the weight tired Gem, exhausted begin him to drop to his knees once again. The edge of the cliff seemed so far away. An insurmountable journey.

"You have touched us all."

Gem looked towards the voice, full of sugar and music and wisdom.

A sparkle of light in a darkening world, a pair of ruby eyes buried deep in a glittering skull. A scribe faerie reached out her hand and touched Gem's chest, then brought her slender fingers to her plump lips before floating back towards her flock. Scribe faeries, hundreds of them, quills and scratchpads and journals clutched in tiny fingers, living moons hovering over the fields. The chanted as their incandescent wings fluttered, ruffling the feathers on their quills.

Mentor. Entertainer.

The wee faeries sputtered, sinking to the ground as the weight on Gem's chest lightened once again.

And Gem pressed on, passing trees and fields of spun gold and greens, babbling brooks and rustling leaves, until his boots landed on the rock overlooking his land. A kingdom, a rainbow of experience, rolled and rippled out as far as the eye could see. His chest swelled with pride at all he had accomplished, all he had built. But his eyes welled too, and the stone in his chest still bore enough weight to keep his spirits pinned to the ground.

"I ain't ready," Gem said, turning his face to the creature, his lip quivering ever so slightly.

A hand, powerful and sensual, rested upon his shoulder.

Gem turned.

"My love," he said.

His queen, Brenda the strong, dressed in a gown of red and gold, its train shimmering for miles over the fertile ground. On the billowing fabric stood his kin, eyes full of pride and adoration, in anticipation of his next journey.

"There are such adventures for you to have," the Queen said, her eyes brimming with love and loss. "You have lived all the tales here, my King. Time to fertilize new lands."

The Queen's crimson heels sunk into the earth as the weight dissolved from Gem's chest, lightening him to the puff of a feather. Her face remained stoic and sure, and her ruby lips pressed against his pallid cheek.

"I can't wait to hear all about your new adventures."

Gem was light as a feather. The heaviness gone, the ambivalence banished, he turned to the creature.

"All right, ye sick ol' bitch. Let's get 'er done."

The creature bowed, a rare expression of respect, and held its arm out over the cliff. A thunderous gnashing of wings echoed through the valley, and the crowd behind Gem cowered to the ground, driven down by fear and the pressure of swirling air. A Puka, pearly white with mane and tail of gold, diamond wings cutting the air like feathered blades, landed on the cliff beside the dark creature.

The Puka knelt in the dirt, and the dark creature held out its hand. Gem stuck out his chin and grasped the hand, and the dark creature hoisted Gem aboard the Puka's massive back. It stood, and Gem towered above his lands, and his people. He looked back into a sea of moist eyes.

"To be continued," Gem said.

He slapped the Puka on the ass and flew off into the silver clouds.

WHY

"Why do you write?"

I could feel her eyes boring into me, doe-brown, young and curious, hungry for her words to find a page of their own.

I breathed in deep, mind blank for a response.

If only I could write her answer, then the cat would relinquish its hold on my tongue.

The smell of parchment wafted into my nose, the buffet of olfactory deliciousness calming my nerves. I looked around, searching for an answer on bookshelves stacked ceiling high with books old and new, papers fretted and yellow or crisp ivory. My eyes found their doppelgänger; a photograph of me holding my newest novel stared back from the foam poster board upon an easel beside my table.

Book signing today, it announced. ***Best-Selling Author***

I looked along the line of people, still searching for an answer to her question.

Why?

My search led me to a little girl near the end of the line, her shoes bedazzled with plastic gems and rubber unicorns...

There I was, standing in the patchy grass outside my elementary school in my own character shoes—Jem, I think—listening to gales of laughter.

Loser, they said, fingers pointed.

Nerd, they cawed as I twirled a strand from the ginger mass of hair atop my head.

At home, beneath my desk, with my notebook lit only by the blue glow of my aquarium, I took out my pencil and silenced them all. My pencil spewed a version of me that was admired, was powerful, was heard; a me whose glorious ginger tresses flowed over the land, gagging down the throats and spilling out of the eye sockets and ears of anyone who dared taunt me...

Then I became a girl, no longer a child but still a few years of experience away from being a woman. A party, my mouth tacky and sickly sweet with the taste of cherry whiskey, and an upstairs bedroom rank with stale smoke. His hands all over me, awkward and rushed, knobby and selfish. I cried the whole way home. When I got there, I grabbed the journal from my desk and plunked myself in the corner of the room. There, lit by the light of the moon, I created a Roman palace, rose petals and soft hands, the smell of fragrant spice and chocolate filling the air, satin sheets and perfect rhythm enticing me to climax...

Suddenly I am a woman, sitting at the park, the midday sun warming my gently aging flesh while my child plays nearby. The wee one comes over for a sip of water, then resumes his play. "Only one?" another mother asks me. I nod. Her judgment sears me to a crisp. "Shame," she says, clucking her tongue.

It had been a long day. A long decade. A string of judgment about motherhood, my career, my appearance, my words, my body. A partner who was absent at best and abusive at worst. My days were spent questioning every choice I had made, would make, or might never have the chance to make.

We left the park. I fed my spawn, tucked him into his nest for the night with a light kiss on the cheek, then went into my office. I had long since traded my pen for a keyboard. I pounded the keys, every tick a beat from my heart.

More kids? Sure, Sally. I wrote myself pregnant, then gave birth to a thousand babies, each one tiny and crimson with rows of sharp, black teeth and long, leathery tongues. They followed me like a swarm, flaying and scalping and devouring anyone and everyone who dared cut me down...

"Ma'am?"

I was still staring at the bedazzled shoes. Everyone in the line was staring at me, silent, waiting. A few whispered to each other, some snickered.

"Why do I write?" I said, breathing out the aroma of books I had been holding in my lungs and heart.

"To survive."

ACKNOWLEDGMENTS

This book would not have been possible without Jessica Raney. I sat across from her Thursday nights at Denny's. Her very presence motivated and inspired me to write. She keeps me focused, helps me when I'm stuck, cleans up my messes, and makes me smile when I feel homicidal. Jess is quite simply the best human and friend I could have ever imagined having in my life. We. Are. Razer. #LDM4evah

To my critique group (that shall not be named): you guys rock. You told me when I was being an idiot, helped me find other words, and have made me a better writer. Thanks for everything.

Jae Mazer is a Canadian who was born in Victoria, British Columbia, and grew up in the prairies of Northern Alberta. After spending the majority of her life battling sasquatches in the Great White North, she migrated south to Texas to have a go at the armadillos. Now she enjoys life as a mom, a musician, and a connoisseur and creator of horror, science fiction, and fantasy. Many moons ago, a rampant love of reading led her to believe she could weave a good tale herself, and she now has seven novels under her belt, as well as short stories published in various anthologies.

CHECK OUT THESE TITLES FROM INKLINGS
PUBLISHING:

The Twisted Reveries Series by Meg Hafdahl debuted in
October 2015 with *Thirteen Tales of the Macabre*. In October
2016, *Tales from Willoughby* followed.

Get your copy of these spine-tingling volumes today and enjoy short stories by this great female voice in horror!

Begin the tale of Willoughby in Meg Hafdahl's debut novel, *Her Dark Inheritance*. Follow Daphne as she uncovers the secrets her mother kept from her for all her life. Just how deeply into Willoughby's dark history do those secrets tie?

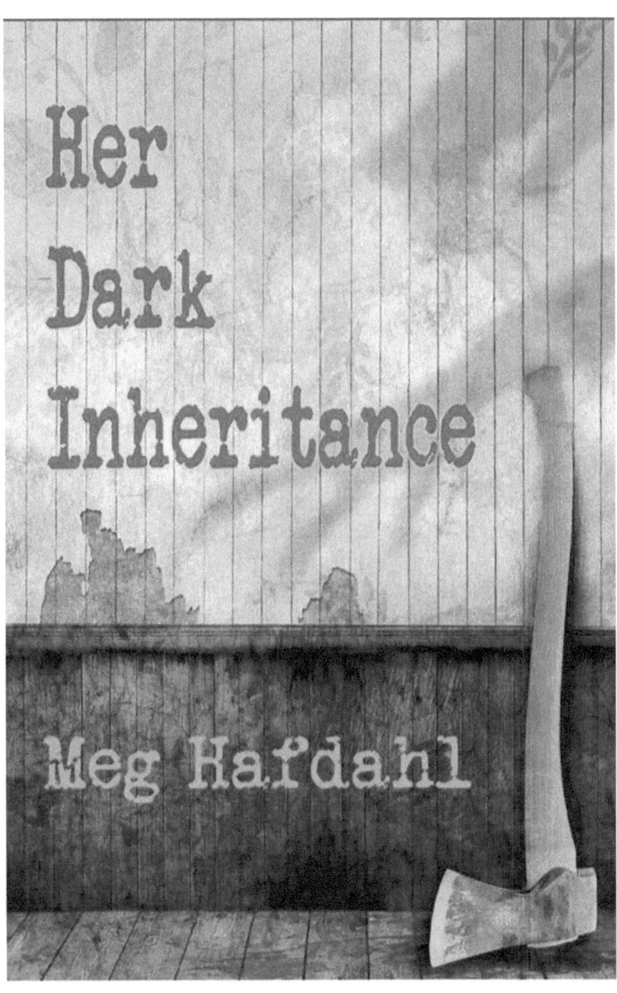